The garden is invaded!

There it was, right before my eyes. I stopped in my tracks and . . . well, Drover ran into me. He always does that when we're in Marching Formation. I stop suddenly and he runs into me. It really burns me up, but on this occasion I was too shocked and amazed to react to Drover's blundering.

"Holy smokes, Drover, do you see what I see?"

"Well, I saw your tail section. It stopped all of a sudden and . . ."

"Never mind the small stuff, son. What I'm seeing up ahead is deadly serious."

"I'll be derned. I wonder what it could be."

I pointed a paw at the garden fence. "Look at that. Someone or something has burrowed under the garden fence!"

"Oh yeah. I wrote a report about that." He sat down and began scratching his left ear. "I think I wrote a report about that. Did I?"

"You wrote a report that was worthless. Why didn't you bring me this information the instant you found it?"

"Well, I was busy . . . I guess."

"Never mind. And stop scratching on the job. Let's move forward and study the crime scene."

The Case of
the Burrowing Robot

The Case of
the Burrowing Robot

John R. Erickson

Illustrations by Gerald L. Holmes

Puffin Books

PUFFIN BOOKS
Published by the Penguin Group
Penguin Putnam Books for Young Readers,
345 Hudson Street, New York, New York 10014, U.S.A.
Penguin Books Ltd,
80 Strand, London WC2R ORL, England
Penguin Books Australia Ltd, 250 Camberwell Road,
Camberwell, Victoria 3124, Australia
Penguin Books Canada Ltd,
10 Alcorn Avenue, Toronto, Ontario, Canada M4V 3B2
Penguin Books (N.Z.) Ltd,
182-190 Wairau Road, Auckland 10, New Zealand

Penguin Books Ltd, Registered Offices:
Harmondsworth, Middlesex, England

Published simultaneously by Viking and Puffin Books,
divisions of Penguin Putnam Books for Young Readers, 2003

9 10 8

LIBRARY OF CONGRESS CATALOGING-IN-PUBLICATION DATA
Erickson, John R.
The case of the burrowing robot / John R. Erickson ;
illustrated by Gerald L. Holmes.
p. cm. — (Hank the cowdog ; 42)
Summary: Hank the Cowdog, Head of Ranch Security, uses his keen detective
skills to find the ruffian responsible for digging holes in Sally May's garden.
ISBN 0-670-03632-3 — ISBN-13: 978-0-14-250063-7 (pbk.)
[1. Dogs—Fiction. 2. Ranch life—West (U.S.)—Fiction. 3. West (U.S.)—Fiction.
4. Humorous stories. 5. Mystery and detective stories.]
I. Holmes, Gerald L., ill. II. Title.

PZ7.E72556Cacd 2003
[Fic]—dc21   2002036984

For Nathaniel Bennett Hobson,
a future fan of the Hank books which are
edited by his mother, Kristin Gilson

CONTENTS

Mechanical
Geniuses at Work

I t's me again, Hank the Cowdog. Everything about
The Case of the Burrowing Robot was strange.
It started strangely and it ended strangely, and in
between it was . . . well, strange.

And scary, very scary. This one will test your
courage.

It began one dark night toward the end of . . .
was it April? Yes, April. I remember it well, because
"April" spelled backward becomes "Lirpa."

In the Security Business, we often spell important words backward to confuse our enemies. Have
we mentioned this? Maybe not, but it's true. It
drives 'em nuts, heh heh, which is exactly where
we want to drive 'em.

See, we've suspected for a long time that they

sometimes plant secret listening devices in our headquarters compound. Once in place, these sensitive devices can pick up Top Secret conversations between and among the elite troops of the Security Division.

You can imagine how serious this could be. Why, if our codes and plans fell into the wrong hands . . . well, it could lead to terrible things, things so grave and dangerous that I'm not even allowed to discuss them. Sorry.

Where were we? Oh yes, The Case of the So Forth. It all began one morning in Lirpa. I had been out doing a routine patrol of the headquarters compound, when all at once I became aware of . . .

Wait, hold everything. *Lirpa*? What the heck does that mean? Hang on a second, we need to check this out.

Hmmmmm.

Data Control shows no listing for "Lirpa." According to our files and records, it's not a real word. Nor is it the name of any known animal, vegetable, or mineral. So what is this non-word, non-name doing in a classified report of The Burrowing Robot?

This could be serious. Can I speak openly and honestly about this? Might as well. Okay, here's the deal. Our enemies are very cunning and sometimes they try to confuse us by introducing garbage words into our communication systems. Perhaps they know that garbage words foul up our systems and that without proper communication, communication is virtually impossible.

When our language is reduced to garbage, everything we say is nothing but rubbish.

So, yes, what we have here is an attempt on the part of our . . . wait a minute, hold everything. Weren't we just talking about . . . ?

Okay, forget the Security Alert. Remember that business about reversing important names and so forth? Lirpa instead of April? Ha ha. You might say that we stepped in our own . . .

Skip it.

The mystery began one warm afternoon around the middle of April, and never mind all that stuff about trying to confuse our enemies. I had just finished checking out a couple of unauthorized sparrows in our elm trees and was on my way back to the office, when I noticed something odd.

I caught a glimpse of High Loper, the owner of this ranch . . . well, he *thinks* he owns it, and most of the time we dogs play along with the illusion. It works better when the people around here think they're in charge, but we dogs know the real story.

(*We're* running things, if you want to know the truth.)

We give the humans little jobs to keep them happy, don't you see, and on that particular afternoon I noticed Loper preparing himself for one of those little jobs. Sally May had been hinting that it was time for him to plow up her garden. After the hints had failed, she had *announced* that it was time for him to so forth, and I found him in front of the shed, glaring down at the dusty Rototiller, which had sat in the machine shed all winter.

He didn't look happy at all. He bent over and blew the dust off the top of the engine, but most of the dust came back in his face, causing him to cough and mutter.

He took hold of the starter rope and gave it a pull. The motor chugged but didn't start. He adjusted the choke and gave the rope another pull. Same deal. It chugged but didn't start. He continued pulling the rope for five long minutes. By then his face had turned a deep shade of red and he was talking out loud to the tiller.

"Stupid pig-nose cantankerous dysfunctional piece of junk!" He kicked the tiller with his left foot. Right foot. Who cares? "Junk!"

Just then, Slim appeared, wearing a little grin. "What's up?"

4

"Garden time."

"How fun."

"You want to do it?"

"Well, I'd love to, Loper, but I'm real busy. And I think Sally May kind of likes your special touch."

"Very funny."

Slim craned his neck and looked at the machine. "How's it going?"

"How do you think it's going?"

Slim's body slumped against the side of the shed and he moved his toothpick to the other side of his mouth. "Not too swell, I'd say. Maybe you ought to kick it again. Sometimes it takes two kicks."

"Sometimes a man should keep his mouth shut."

Slim tried to look serious. "What seems to be the problem?"

Loper heaved a sigh and looked up at the sky. "Slim, if I knew the problem, I'd fix it. It won't start."

"I don't reckon you bothered to check the gas tank. These motors run better when they've got gas."

Loper stared at him. "Am I stupid? Do I look stupid?"

"Well, now, that's a matter of opinion, I reckon, but the truth is that sometimes you *don't* check the gas."

"Once. I did that once, and it was so long ago, nobody remembers it. Nobody but you, that is. Half the time, you can't remember which boot goes on which foot, but you'll never forget the *one time* I forgot to check the gas."

"You've done it many times, Loper. You just slam-bang your way into these deals and then throw a little fit when the thing won't start. If you ask me, that's pretty childish, a grown man yelling and carrying on. And kicking the poor machine. How'd you like to be a garden tiller and have some yahoo kick you first thing in the morning?"

Loper studied him for a long moment. "You know, Slim, if somebody didn't know better, he might think you're some kind of hotshot mechanic."

Slim raised his chin. "I've made a few turns with a wrench, and if I do say so myself, I've bailed you out of more than one mess."

"Oh, you have, huh?"

"Yes sir, I sure have, and the reason is that you've got no more patience than a teenage boy during a full moon."

"Is that so?"

"That's so. We've got raccoons on this ranch that would make better mechanics than you."

A wicked smile slithered across Loper's mouth.

"What are you saying? Are we drifting toward some kind of friendly wager?"

"Not friendly."

"How much?"

Slim hitched up his jeans. "Five bucks says I'll have this tiller throwing up dirt in thirty minutes. You just run along and find some little job to keep you out of my hair, and I'll do the rest."

"By grabs, I'll take that bet." Loper waved good-bye and started walking toward the corrals. "See you in half an hour."

"Good deal. And bring cash. We don't take checks or credit cards." When Loper had gone, Slim gave me a wink. "Heh. He never checks the gas. Watch this, pooch."

He unscrewed the lid of the gas tank and poked a finger into the opening. His smile faded. When he brought it out, the finger was dripping gasoline. He wiped it on his jeans and said, "I'll be derned. He checked the gas. I guess we'll go straight into Plan B."

He took the starter rope in his hand and gave it a pull. Again and again. Minutes passed. The motor turned over but didn't start.

Twenty minutes later, Slim had shucked off his hat and shirt. Sweat dripped off the end of his nose and his face had turned a dangerous shade

of red. He stretched a kink out of his back and started screaming at the tiller.

"Contrary machine! Moron! Dadgum frazzling modern contraption!" Then, before my very eyes, he *kicked* the tiller. "All right, by netties, you asked for this. I'm fixing to give you open-carburetor surgery, and if you die on the operating table, I'll personally haul you to the junk yard."

With that, he stomped into the machine shed and stomped back outside with a handful of wrenches and other tools. He bent over the machine and was about to begin the surgery, when Sally May walked up. I guess she'd heard all the screaming and wondered what was going on.

She stood there for a moment, looking over Slim's shoulder. "It won't start?" Slim was too mad to speak. "Didn't we have this problem last year?" Slim grunted and went on working. "What was the problem last year? Oh, some little valve or gizmo on the gas line. Somebody had shut off the valve."

Slim's head drifted up. He cut his eyes from side to side. "That ain't it, Sally May, I already checked."

She smiled and shrugged and went back down to the house. Slim watched her leave. When she reached the yard gate and was too far away to see what he was doing, he slipped his fingers under the carburetor and turned a little valve. Then he reeled his watch out of his pocket and checked the time.

A smile spread across his mouth and he yelled, "Loper! Come get your tiller!" Then he looked down at me and chuckled. "Heh. Clean living and patience have triumphed again, pooch."

Loper arrived moments later. Slim pointed to the machine and said, "Give 'er a twirl and see what she says."

Loper stepped up to the machine and pulled on the starter rope. It chugged on the first pull, and started running on the second. Loper scowled, shook his head, muttered, pulled out his wallet, and shut off the machine.

He handed five bucks over to Slim. "Here. May it bring you misery. What did you do?"

"Oh, not much. Overhauled the carburetor, blew out the lines, changed out the piston rings, replaced the head gasket. Thanks, Loper. We sure appreciate your business."

Slim flashed a grin and stuffed the money into his pocket.

Loper was silent for a moment. "Slim, suppose you've got two men standing side by side. How can you tell which is the boss and which is the hired hand?"

"Well, let's see. The hired hand's handsomer and looks quite a bit smarter?"

Loper shook his head. "Nope. The boss is the one who goes to town on an errand, and the hired hand's the one who plows the garden."

Slim's smile died. "Now hold on . . ."

Loper patted him on the shoulder. "I don't know how you started that thing, buddy, but it was some kind of crooked deal. Never cheat the boss, Slim. Have a great day."

Then, whistling a tune, Loper hiked over to his pickup and drove away.

CHAPTER TWO

The Sharing
of Pain

That left me and Slim standing there alone.
Slim's face had settled into a wad of sour lines.
I could see that this was turning into a Sharing the
Pain situation, so I switched my tail over to Slow
Taps, and even tried to squeeze up a few tears.

I mean, this was a sad time, right? Slim had
succeeded in his mission of starting the stubborn
machine, yet Loper had . . . to be honest, my attention had wandered and I wasn't really sure what
had happened, but of this I was sure: Slim's for-
tunes had taken a dive and he looked unhappy,
very unhappy.

Every unhappy master needs an unhappy dog.
That's the whole concept behind the Sharing of
Pain. By George, if Slim's mood had just fallen

into the Toilet of Life, the least I could do . . .

By the way, were you aware that we have a song for The Sharing of Pain? We do, and I happen to know it. Here's how it goes.

The Sharing of Pain

The sharing of pain is always a strain.
It causes a huge emotional drain.
You've got to look bleak.
It's not for the weak.
This little racket pays off even better than gold,
If you're bold . . . enough.

You start with a face that mirrors the boss.
Then you can add emotional sauce.
You moan when he moans,
You groan when he groans,
Then there's a bonus that comes if you shed
   a few tears,
That can smear . . . your face.

The tiniest signs can add good effect:
A quivering lip says, "Life is a wreck."
Slow Taps on the tail,
A whimpering wail
All tell him your heart is in danger of
   breaking in two.
And it's true . . . almost.

13

The sharing of pain could drive you insane.
You suffer and grieve, and what do you gain?
Just think of the cost
Of pleasing the boss!
But if you're lucky the payoff will come, and
　　perhaps . . .
Double scraps . . . tonight!

The sharing of pain . . .

Pretty impressive, huh? You bet. Yes sir, great song, and there is no better form of job security than a good convincing Boo Hoo Program, and I went right to work on it. I dimmed the eyes, lowered the head to an angle of about 23 degrees, and set the ears in the Big Droop Position.

Yes, this was a very sad moment for the ranch. Our hearts were broken. Or nearly broken. If not broken, they were certainly cracked and damaged.

I turned my sad eyes on Slim and waited for my next cue.

He . . . huh? He grinned and patted his wallet. "Well, I have to plow the garden, but by grabs, I got five dollars of Loper's money. Tight as he is, he'll brood on that for two weeks, and I'll never tell him the scientific miracle for starting tillers." He gave me a wink and whispered, "You open the gas valve."

So . . . we were happy again? We had passed through the Vale of Sorrow and Anger? Yes, it appeared that all was well and life was good again. In a flash, I turned to the control panel of my mind and began throwing switches. OFF went Big Droop, Slow Taps, Sharing of Pain, Toilet of Life, and Boo Hoo, and ON went Joyous Leaps, Wide Grins, and Exuberant Swings on the tail section.

Oh happy day! We had won five bucks in a wager! Our ship had come in, and peace and tranquittery had returned to the ranch!

I was in the midst of this wild celebration, when I realized that Drover had wandered into the scenery and was staring at me. He twisted his head to the side and gave me a puzzled look.

"What's all the excitement about?"

"It's about joy, Drover, wild unfettered joy."

"I'll be derned. What's unfeathered joy?"

"It's the opposite of fettered joy. The *un-* means 'not.'"

"I'll be derned. So an onion's not really a veg-etable?"

"That's correct. It's common knowledge that onions cause crying, so an onion is the opposite of joy. Do you see how it all fits together?"

"So . . . an onion is really a feather?"

"Yes, exactly. The only question remaining is,

why are you just standing there?" He sat down. "Why are you just sitting there?" He stood up. "Drover, the point I'm trying to make is that Slim and I are in the midst of a wild celebration."

"Yeah, I noticed."

"Then why aren't you celebrating? The whole ranch is filled with joy, yet you're just standing there."

"Well . . . what are you celebrating?"

"We're celebrating . . . it doesn't matter, Drover. This is Slim's deal. He won five bucks and gets to plow the garden. It's not necessary that we understand every detail. What matters is that we're happy."

Drover seemed confused. "He's going to use five deer to plow the garden?"

I interrupted my Leaps of Joy and stomped over to the runt. "He won five *dollars* in a wager and is going to plow the garden with the tiller. There are no deer."

"I saw two bucks and a doe this morning, down by the creek. You said there weren't any deer."

"I said . . . Drover, forget the deer, forget the dollars. The point here is that we're in the midst of an important celebration. Slim is happy, and it's our job as dogs to share in that happiness. Do you suppose you could trouble yourself to show some happiness?"

"Well . . . I guess I could try. What should I do?"

"Jump up and down. Smile. Wag your tail in a vigorous manner."

"I don't have a tail."

"That's true. Okay, wiggle your stub in a vigorous manner. Give it a shot."

"Okay, here I go." He began jumping up and down, grinning, and wiggling his stub tail. Oh, and he started yipping: "Happy, happy, happy! How'm I doing?"

I studied him with a critical eye. "Not bad. Pretty good. I'm impressed, Drover. See what you can do when you put your mind to it?"

"Yeah, I'm really happy now!"

Well, now that I'd gotten Drover going in the right direction, I plunged myself back into Joyous Leaps and . . .

Huh?

Slim wasn't smiling any more. His face had returned to its previous expression of . . . something. Sourness, darkness, depression. Sadness, heartbreak, woe. He turned toward the tiller and said, "But now I have to run this bucking machine and plow the stinking garden—just what every cowboy loves to do on a pretty spring day. Baloney!"

He cranked up the motor, seized the handles, and started driving the tiller toward the . . .

HUH?

"Out of the road, dogs, or you'll be sausage! Once I get started, I ain't slowing down for man nor beets!"

Sure, fine. But he might have at least . . . I shut down all the Joy circuits and yelled, "Drover, we're out of the Joy Program now!"

"Happy, happy, happy!"

"Drover, the happy is over!"

He didn't hear me. He kept hopping up and down, grinning like a lunatic, and squeaking, "Happy, happy, happy!"

I had no choice but to give him Growls and Fangs. "Quit hopping around! You look like an idiot."

He stopped and stared at me. "I was just being happy."

"I understand that you were being happy, but the happy times are over. We've just gotten fresh orders. We're back to the Sharing of Pain."

"Pain? I just started being happy."

"Life has many ups and downs, Drover, and we dogs don't write the script. Now, get into the Boo Hoo Program and let's escort Slim down to the garden. He's going to need lots of help on this deal."

In a matter of seconds, we reconfigured all switches and circuits and technobobbery, and transformed ourselves into Figures of Gloom. Pretty impressive, huh? You bet. I mean, how many dogs in this world can make those huge adjustments in such a short time? Not many. But we did.

Like black Cadillacs in a funeral procession, we escorted poor Slim down to the cemetery of his garden plot. It was a sad procession. Our eyes were vacant. Our heads hung low. Our ears lay flat and

lifeless on our heads. Our tails were in the OFF position, and mine even dragged the ground. (Drover's didn't, for obvious reasons.)

When we reached the garden area, we dogs took up a Mourning Position beneath a big elm tree, and watched.

Slim maneuvered the tiller through the gate and started plowing. Have you ever seen someone operating a garden tiller? If the ground happens to be hard, the tiller bucks and kicks, whilst the operator hangs on to the handlebars and tries to keep the thing in an upright position.

It was hard work. I could see that it was wearing poor Slim down. I mean, he was dripping sweat and muttering hateful things under his breath. Minutes passed. An hour. More minutes passed. The temperature began to rise.

A lot of your ordinary dogs would have quit, abandoned their master, shut off Boo Hoo, and gone somewhere to take a nap. Not us, fellers. We were the elite snorks of the . . . the elite troops of the Slurry Divizzzzzzzz . . . the elite troops of the Security Division, shall we say, and sleeping wasn't an option for uzzzzzzzzzzzzzzzzzzzzzz . . .

. . . wasn't an option for us. We had a job to do, an important job, and that job required that we stay awhop and alurk . . . awake and alert, that is.

20

Yes, the temptation to drift off into . . . snerk, muff, mork, honky wigglewort . . .

. . . the temptation to drift off into sleep was very powdery, but so was our sniss of loyalburble to our . . . zzzzzzzzzzzzzzzzzzzzzzzzzzzzzzzzzzzzzzzzz zzzzzzzzzzzzzzzzzzzzzzzzzzz.

CHAPTER THREE

Slim's Garden Ordeal

Perhaps you're wondering what all this business of plowing up the garden has to do with the Case of the Burrowing Robot. The answer is . . . *plenty*. At this point, you don't understand the connection, but I'll give you a little hint.

No, I won't give you any hints. You'll just have to be patient and keep reading. And try to show some confidence in the guy who's telling this story. Don't forget, I'm Head of Ranch Security.

Now, where were we? Oh yes, wide-awake near the garden, sharing the pain of Slim's ordeal, and . . .

Okay, maybe we drifted off to sleep, but let me hasten to add that Drover was the first to fall to temptation, and the sound of his snoring . . . well, it corrupted me in small but tiny ways. If it hadn't

22

been for Drover, if I'd been there by myself . . .

Hey, who wouldn't have fallen asleep? A dog can Share Pain for so long and then it gets *really boring*, especially when it involves watching some guy plow up a garden. Five minutes would have been about right, but this deal went on for two whole hours! Three whole hours. I lost track of the time because I fell asl—because I didn't have a watch.

Dogs don't carry watches.

It went on for three or four hours, and who's going to stay awake for that? Not me. I fought sleep as long as I could, and finally it just dragged me down. But notice that I didn't leave. No sir, I stayed right there with my master and did my sleeping on the job site.

No ordinary dog could have done that.

I was awakened from slumberous sleep by the sound of . . . something. Footsteps? Voices? The squeak of gate hinges? I rushed to the window of my mind and raised the curtains. There before me, inside the garden fence, were three humanoid forms: one tall, one short, and one middle-sized. They appeared to be performing some kind of labor that involved rakes and hoes.

Naturally, my first thought was that our ranch had been invaded by humanoid life forms from another galaxy. I mean, I didn't recognize them and they looked pretty suspicious out there, hacking around in our garden with strange instruments, so I sounded the alarm.

Yes sir, I barked. When in doubt, bark first and ask questions later. That's what I always say. I threw myself into the task and fired off five or six blasts of . . . huh? Okay, we cancelled the alert.

False alarm. You'll never guess who that was out there in the garden.

Ha ha.

Slim, Sally May, and Little Alfred. Ha ha. They were all working in the garden, see. Raking, hoeing up rows, planting seeds, and transplanting various kinds of vegetable life forms, such as your tomato plants and your pepper plants and your so forths.

Furthermore, it appeared that they had been laboring for quite a while and were almost finished. Heck, the evening shadows had grown long and we were approaching the sunset period of the day, which occurs ever day around sunset.

This provided me with an important clue: Drover had slept through the whole thing. I made a mental note to give him a stern lecture about sleeping on the job and being a half-stepper, but just then the workers emerged from the garden area. A quick sweep of their faces told me they were tired, but proud of a job well done.

Sally May said, "Thanks, Slim. I know this isn't your favorite kind of work, but I sure appreciate it. You did a good job with the tiller."

"Yeah, and it's done a pretty good job on me too. That thing will shake your gizzard loose." At that very moment, Slim's eyes swung around and landed on . . . well, on ME, you might say. And he said—this is an exact quote—he said, "Pooch, I know you'll be tempted to get in there and dig around in that fresh dirt. I'd urge you not to do that, hear? 'Cause if you just can't resist the temptation, I'm liable to kick your little doggie tail up between your ears."

Sally May nodded, "That's right, Hank. *No dogs in the garden.*"

And then Little Alfred said, "Don't dig in our garden, Hankie."

Huh? Me? What was this? No dogs in the . . . hey, did they need to tell me *that*? I mean, they weren't talking to chopped liver. I was Head of Ranch Security, right? I knew about hard work and garden plants and all that other stuff, and the very idea that they would . . .

I hadn't done anything wrong. I hadn't even thought about doing anything wrong. In fact, I had spent the entire afternoon . . . *wasted* the entire afternoon, it appeared, trying to be a good loyal dog, sharing the pain of Slim's Garden Ordeal. Had anyone noticed that? Had I gotten any points for loyalty and devotion to duty? Was anyone rushing over to me with Double Scraps? Heck no.

Sometimes I wonder what it takes to please these people. You give them your best and they want more. You give them a pint of blood and they want 500 gallons. You give them . . .

Okay, fine. They could insult me if they wanted, but I didn't have to sit there and take it. "Sticks and stones may break my bones, but I can always leave." And that's just what I did. Before their very eyes, their very astonished eyes, I heaved myself up to an upright position, pointed my nose high in the air, and marched away, leaving them weeping and crying and regretting all the hateful charges they'd brought against me.

Too bad. It served 'em right. I had better things to do with my life, such as . . . okay, maybe I didn't exactly have a lot of interesting projects lined up for the rest of the day, but I could find things to do that didn't involve . . .

Oh, by the way, you might be wondering what became of Drover whilst I was being screeched at, glared at, and lectured. Well, he just . . . vanished. He does this all the time. At the first sound of a raised voice or a loud noise, he disappears. I don't know how he does it, the little weenie, but one of these days . . . oh well.

Where were we? Just the very thought of Drover gets me confused. Oh yes, the garden. We plowed and planted the garden on a Monday afternoon. Three days later . . . let's see, it must have been during the early morning hours of Friday, I was in my office on the twelfth floor of the Security Division's Vast Office Complex. While the rest of the world slept on this dark night, I found myself all alone, reading over a huge stack of . . .

Wait. I wasn't alone. Drover was there too, sleeping his life away on his gunnysack bed on the floor. As usual, he was twitching, wheezing, and making an incredible orchestra of sounds in his sleep.

Anyway, I found myself reading over a weird report. Drover had turned it in that very afternoon. It didn't add up, it didn't make sense. Would you care to take a peek at it? We're not supposed to show these reports to anyone outside of the Security Division, no kidding, but on the other hand . . . who's going to know?

I guess it wouldn't hurt, just this once. But don't be blabbing this stuff around. Here it is, Secret Report #394959-333, written in Drover's own words:

My Report

by Drover Dog

Well, let's see here. I was walking around. The sun was shining. It was pretty hot and I got a drink. A bird flew past and landed in a tree. I saw two crickets and a grasshopper, and then I saw one grasshopper and two crickets.

Maybe they were the same ones. I get confused sometimes.

And then I walked around some more. Life gets kind of boring on hot days. I've always liked winter better than summer. Summertime always seems so hot.

We're still in the month of April and it's not summertime yet, but I still say that summer is too hot.

Oh yeah, and that's when I saw it. Boy, I was shocked. I wondered who did such a terrible thing.

Anyway, that's my report.

There. You see what I mean about it being a weird report? It was rubbish! It was impossible to tell if the runt had actually seen something important, or if he'd just been waltzing around headquarters, muttering to himself.

I decided to get to the bottom of this. "Drover,

wake up. We need to discuss this report you turned in." He twitched and squeaked. "Drover, I'm giving you a direct order. Wake up this very moment!"

His head shot up. Two eyes filled with a great emptiness stared at me. His ears were set at different angles, one pointing upward and the other pointing east. And then he said—this is a direct quote—he said, "Oh, hi. We're away from the foam

right now. Just leave a mess and we'll go back to sleep. Honk, snerf, zzzzzz."

And with that, his eyes slammed shut and he collapsed back into the gravitational pull of his gunnysack. Was I going to sit there and take that for an answer? No sir. I pushed myself up from my cluttered desk and rumbled over to his potsrate body. I placed my mouth right next to the flap of his left ear and went into a little routine we call, heh heh, "Railroad Crossing/Train Coming."

HONNNNNK!

Heh heh. It got his attention. He jumped two feet into the air, and when he hit the ground again, his eyes were wide open. "Help, murder, Mayday! The train's coming! Oh my leg!" He stared at me for a long moment. "Oh, hi. Did you see that train?"

"There's no train, Drover. I was merely trying to wake you up, and I was forced to use my Train Horn application."

His eyes darted from side to side. "No, this was a real train. I saw it myself."

I heaved a sigh. "Drover, I repeat. There was no train."

"Then . . . then what was that thing I saw?"

"I have no idea. Describe it."

"Well, let's see here. It was this huge thing

made of iron and steel. It had wheels instead of legs, and ..."

"Wait a minute, hold everything. You say it had *wheels*? Describe the wheels."

"Well, they were ... round. And they were turning."

"Hmmm. Round ... turning. This is interesting, Drover, because the objects you've just described fit our profiles of ... wheels. Were you aware of that? Go on, tell me more."

"Well, it blew its horn and then ... and it said ... choo, choo!"

I stared into the vacuum of his eyes. "Choo choo? Are you serious?"

I began pacing back and forth in front of him, as I often do when my mind is racing. Drover was on to something here, and I had to find out exactly what it was.

I didn't want to leap to any pasty conclusions, but it certainly appeared that we had an *enemy train running loose on the ranch*!

The Bogus Enemy Train Report

The tension inside our office grew tensioner and tensionest. "All right, Drover, tell me more. When and where did you observe this thing?"

"Well, let me think here. I was . . . sitting in the middle of some tracks."

"Ah, tracks! Now we're cooking. Describe them. Were they coyote tracks, dog tracks, cat tracks . . . what kind of tracks? This could be crucial."

"Well, let's see. They weren't coyote tracks, I'm pretty sure, 'cause there were two of 'em and they were made out of . . . steel."

I stopped pacing and studied the runt with narrowed eyes. Let me rephrase that. With narrowed eyes, I studied the runt. "Tracks? Made of steel? Two steel tracks, running parallel and side by side?"

"Yeah, but how'd you know that?"

I gave him a smirk. "I know, Drover, because you've just blown this case wide open. Don't you get it?"

"Well . . ."

"Wheels, whistle, choo choo, two tracks made of steel, running side by side . . . it all adds up to one thing. What you saw, Drover, was a train! Before, we had no hard proof. Now we have it—the tracks!"

"I'll be derned."

"And now we must rush to the next question. Where did you see this train? Here on the ranch?"

"Well, I . . . let me think here."

"Hurry up. We don't have a moment to spare."

"You know . . ." He yawned. "I think maybe I was . . . asleep."

I stopped pacing and froze. "Asleep? What does that have to do with the train? If you were asleep, how could you have observed the train?"

"That's what I mean. Now that I think about it, I think I just . . . dreamed it."

The air hissed out of my lungs and my whole body went limp. "Dreamed it! Are you saying . . ." I marched over to him and stuck my nose in his face. "Drover, minutes ago I woke you up with my Train Horn application. Is it possible that your tiny brain took that sound and transformed it into a bogus report about an enemy train, steaming through the middle of ranch headquarters?"

He gave me a silly grin. "You know, I'll bet that's what happened. Kind of weird, isn't it?"

There was a long, throbbing moment of silence, as I searched the vast sweep of my mind for the proper words to describe . . .

"Drover, word of this conversation must never leak out to the world at large. We have just spent the past five minutes discussing utter nonsense. I don't think the general public would understand."

"No, they'd probably think we're just . . . well, a couple of dumb dogs."

"Exactly." I gave him a pat on the shoulder. "And to avoid any misunderstandings, we're going to, uh, seal this file. No one will ever know."

"Oh good, 'cause . . ."

"Now hush and get out of bed. We have a very important matter to discuss."

Remember Drover's report? I gave you a peek at it, and if you were paying attention, you probably noticed that it contained no facts at all. None. Yet, at the end of the report, Drover had said something like, "Boy, I was shocked that somebody had done such a terrible thing."

See what I mean? No facts, no details, no solid information that you could use for building a case.

If the little mutt had been "shocked" by some "terrible thing," I wanted to know about it.

Well, at last I had Mister Asleep On The Train Tracks wide awake, and I seized this opportunity to probe his tiny mind. I began pacing back and forth in front of him, as I often do when . . . I've already covered that.

I began pacing. "All right, Drover, let's get right down to business. I want to discuss that report of yours."

He yawned. "Gosh, it's kind of late. Could we wait 'til morning?"

"Negative on that. We're in the Security Business. Our work waits on no man."

"Yeah, but we're dogs."

"Tell me about your report."

"Oh drat. Well, let me think here. Oh yeah! I was asleep and then I was awake, and I saw this train coming right toward me."

"Not the train. We've already discussed the train."

"We did?"

"Yes, and there was no train."

"I'll be derned. What about those tracks?"

"There were no tracks. Trains that don't exist leave no tracks."

"What about those tracks down by the garden?"

"Were they train tracks?"

"I don't think so, 'cause you just said that trains don't exist."

I stopped pacing and gave him a glare of purest steel. "I didn't say that trains don't exist. Trains do exist, otherwise there would be no train tracks anywhere in the world."

"Yeah, but they weren't train tracks, I'm pretty sure of that."

"Which tracks are we discussing, Drover? Did you actually see some tracks?"

"Oh yeah, down by the garden. I put it in my report."

I marched over to him. "You didn't put anything about tracks in your report. I read your report. It told me nothing about anything, and it didn't contain one word about tracks."

He grinned. "I'll be derned. Maybe I forgot to mention the tracks. I found some tracks down by the garden."

"Let me get this straight, Drover. You wrote up a report to report on some tracks you found, but you didn't mention the tracks you found in your report?"

"Well . . . I didn't find 'em in the report. They were down by the garden."

"But the tracks were the whole point of your report?"

"Oh yeah, and I found a hole too."

"And you didn't even mention it? Drover, sometimes I think . . . wait a minute, hold everything. Did you just say something about a hole?"

"Well, let me think here . . ."

I stuck my nose in his face and screamed, "You said something about a hole, you little moron! Did you find a hole somewhere?"

He shriveled and began to sniffle. "Don't yell at me! It makes me think you don't like me."

"You're driving me insane, is all. Did you find some tracks and a hole down at the garden? Out with it!"

"Yes, yes, I did! And that's why I wrote the report."

I closed my eyes and took a deep breath of air. "Drover, listen carefully. You wrote a report that said nothing about tracks or a hole in the garden. I read it five times. I know what I'm talking about. For the last time, did you find tracks and a hole?"

He nodded. "Yeah, I was shocked. I knew you'd want to know."

I turned away from the little lunatic. "You knew I'd want to know, so you wrote a report that said nothing about it."

"I guess I forgot."

"I guess you did. Well, never mind, Drover, let's

try to put this behind us. The milk has already been spilled under the bridge."

"No, it was in the garden. Somebody dug a hole in Sally May's garden, and I didn't see a bridge."

I stared at him in disbelief. "What? Somebody dug a hole . . . you found a hole in Sally May's garden?"

He grinned and nodded. "Sure did. Are you proud of me?"

"Drover, do you have any idea how serious this is? Do you know who or whom will be blamed for this? You found evidence of a serious crime, yet in your report . . ."

I paced a few steps away from him and looked up at the stars. For a long moment I tried to unscramble my thought processes. "Drover, may I ask you a personal question?"

"Oh sure, ask me anything. I love to talk at night."

"How long have you been . . . *like this*? I mean, were you odd as a child? Please be honest."

"Well, let me think here." He wadded up his mouth and squinted one eye. "Nope, I was just a normal, happy little dog. And Rupert was my best friend."

"You had a friend named Rupert?"

"Oh yeah. He was my pet bone. We went every-where together."

My eyes rolled up inside my head. "Never mind, Drover, I can't stand any more of this."

"Good old Rupe. I haven't thought about him in years."

"Drover, please shut up and listen. We have reason to suspect that someone or something has been digging holes in Sally May's garden. As you know, that's a very serious offense."

"Yeah, 'cause the fence is made of hog wire."

"On the count of three, we will end this ridiculous conversation about your pet bone and march in formation down to the garden. There, we will conduct a thorough investigation. I would be grateful if you never spoke to me again."

"Gosh, thanks."

"You're welcome. Let's get out of here."

Whew! Somehow, just in the nickering of time, I managed to pull myself out of the swamp of Drover's . . . whatever. I don't even have a word for it. Sometimes, when I talk to the little mutt, I get the feeling . . . never mind.

The Garden Is Invaded!

What matters is that I had managed to drag some very important facts out of Drover, namely that we just might have uncovered a very serious unauthorized entry into Sally May's garden.

Pretty scary, huh? You bet. Sally May can be pretty scary when she's aroused, and I had a feeling that a hole in her precious garden would bring her wrath down upon the entire amassed forces of the Security Division . . . unless, of course, we were able to solve the case and catch the villain.

Solving the case became Job Number One. Everything else went on hold. Daylight would be coming in just a few hours, and if Sally May went down to her garden in the cool of the morning and found . . . gulp. I didn't even want to think about it.

41

See, I knew exactly who would be accused of digging the hole. Me. It wasn't fair, it wasn't right, it wasn't just, but that was the kind of world we lived in—the kind of world where the Head of Ranch Security got blamed for every offense and every unsolved crime.

Why? I couldn't imagine.

Okay, I could imagine, but just barely. See, in the days of my careless youth, I had been drawn to . . . uh . . . certain types of folly. I had yielded to temptation on a few rare occasions . . . maybe we'd better just go straight to the point and blurt it out.

Hang on to something steady, this will come as a shock.

I had in fact dug around in her garden on a few occasions, but that had been long ago, back in the days of my careless youth. Since those days, I had grown into a mature, responsible citizen of the ranch, and had even been promoted to the position of Head of Ranch Security.

Need I say more? I was now on the side of law and order, and was in charge of protecting Sally May's garden from the kind of ruffians and villains who would dig holes in it.

If there really *was* a hole in the garden. Don't forget, this report had come from Drover. I would have to check it out myself. Only then would I believe that he had actually made an important discovery.

We arranged ourselves in Marching Formation and tramped through the darkness, until we came to the garden area. As you may know, it lay to the northeast of the gas tanks (our office complex), about halfway between the tanks and the corrals. As you may also know, it was enclosed within a fairly substantial hog wire fence.

The cowboys must have built the fence on a cool day. How do I know that? Easy. If they'd built it on a hot summer day, it would have turned out to be rickety, not "fairly substantial."

That's a pretty clever line of reasoning, isn't it? Heh. When you work in the Security Business, you notice these tiny dovetails. Details, let us say. We gather up the tiniest of clues, put 'em all together, and then we . . .

HUH?

There it was, right before my very eyes. I stopped in my tracks and . . . well, Drover ran into me. He always does that when we're in Marching Formation. I stop suddenly and he runs into me. It really burns me up, but on this occasion I was too shocked and amazed to react to Drover's blundering.

"Holy smokes, Drover, do you see what I see?"

"Well, I saw your tail section. It stopped all of a sudden and . . ."

"Never mind the small stuff, son. What I'm seeing up ahead is deadly serious."

"I'll be derned. I wonder what it could be."

I pointed a paw at the garden fence. "Look at that. Someone or something has burrowed under the garden fence!"

"Oh yeah. I wrote a report about that." He sat down and began scratching his left ear. "I think I wrote a report about that. Did I?"

"You wrote a report that was worthless. Why didn't you bring me this information the instant you found it?"

"Well, I was busy . . . I guess."

"Never mind. And stop scratching on the job. Let's move forward and study the crime scene."

I crept forward on silent paws, closer and closer, until I was standing right over the alleged hole under the fence. "Well, there it is, son. There can no longer be any doubt or question about it. Someone burrowed under the garden fence. The evidence is indespittable: fresh dirt, odd little tracks in the . . . wait a minute! Fresh dirt?" I whirled around and faced my assistant. "Did you hear that, Drover? *Fresh dirt.*"

"No thanks, I'm stuffed. And I never eat dirt anyway."

"No, no, you missed the point. The dirt we're seeing here is moist and fresh. Do you see what that means?"

"Well, I guess if you ate dirt, you'd want it to be . . . fresh."

I stared at the little goof. "No. It means . . . listen carefully, I don't want to repeat myself . . . it means that the villain has returned . . . and might be in the garden at this very moment."

I heard him gasp. "You mean . . . oh my gosh! You know, Hank, this old leg's sure been acting up. Maybe I'd better . . ."

"Stand your ground, son, we may be very close to a combat situation."

"Help! The pain! Oh my leg!"

"Hush! We're switching all communications over to the Battle Frequency. Your code name for this mission will be Wooden Spoon. Mine will be Plumber's Friend." I turned to the microphone of my mind. "Control, this is Plumber's Friend. We're activating the Emergency System, over." I waited for an answer. "Hello? Control, this is Plumber's Friend, come in, over!" Nothing but static on the line. I turned to Drover. "Drover, something's happened to your eyes. They look like two fried eggs."

"Help! Oh my gosh, Hank, I see something!"

"Shhhh! We're using code names. Do you want the whole world to know who we are?"

"Oh, sorry. What's your code name?"

"I, uh . . . it was right on the tip of my tongue."

Drover squinted his eyes and stared at . . . well, the tip of my tongue, I suppose. "Canker Sore?"

"Right, that's it. Canker Sore. What did you see?"

"Well, let me think here. Oh yeah. Canker Sore, this is Wooden Plumber."

"Hurry up, Drover!"

"I just saw something in the garden! Look over there!"

I tore my gaze away from . . . his eyes really did look like two fried eggs in a skillet, no kidding . . . I tore my gaze away from Drover's skillet face and directed my visual instruments toward the . . .

HUH?

A wave of electrical current shot down my backbone. I couldn't believe this. I was so shocked, I forgot all about Drover's egg-eyes and how much they reminded me of happy Scrap Times at the yard gate.

Hang on to something. This is going to give you a jolt. In fact, we may need to clear the room of all little children. No kidding, this isn't a drill. All little kids must leave . . . NOW.

Are we clear? Okay, here we go. I found myself staring at some *inhuman, unearthly space monster robot*! You think this is a joke? It's not a joke, believe me. It was the real thing. Here, check out the specs on this thing.

Description: sharp pointed nose, beady little eyes, long tail, two small ears, four legs, and sharp claws.

You probably think it was a badger, right? Or maybe a skunk? Ha. Far from it. I know my skunks and my badgers, and this was neither, and here comes the real shocker.

This creature had no hair. That's right, not a

single hair. Instead, it was covered, from head to tail, with *armored plating*, perhaps made of some type of high-tech steel alloy we'd never seen or heard of.

Drover must have noticed all these details too. "Hank, oh my gosh, what is that thing?"

"I'm not sure at this point. My best guess is that it's some kind of . . . burrowing robot. And I don't think it's from Planet Earth."

"Me neither. You know, I'd kind of like to go back to Planet Gunnysack."

"Negatory on that. It's too late. We've found the thing, and now we have to do something."

"Well . . . maybe we could pretend that we didn't find it. I won't tell if you won't."

I gave that some thought. "It's tempting, Drover, and that's just the kind of thing your ordinary dogs would do—hide, go back to bed, make up an elaborate diaper of lies to cover their hineys. But we're the Elite Troops of the Security Division and we have to be just a little bit special."

"I'm especially scared, that's how special I feel."

"I understand, son. One part of me wants to run away and forget the whole incident, but the other part says, 'No, we must see it through to the bitter end.'" I could hear Drover's teeth clacking in the darkness. "Try to be brave. Try to be professional."

"What if I faint?"

"That wouldn't be brave or professional. Don't do it."

I turned my gaze back to the garden and studied the creature again. If it had seen us, it showed no fear or concern. It appeared to be . . . well, just poking around in the fresh dirt, digging with its front paws.

Well, it was time to act. "Drover, I've got to get this report through to Control. Control, this is Wooden Plumber, over. Can you read me? Repeat: *can you read me*? We have a crisis situation in the garden. Repeat: *we have a crisis situation in the garden*! Over."

In the tensionous silence, I waited for Control to come back. Nothing but static. The line went dead.

I turned to my moon-eyed assistant. "Well, Drover, it looks like we're on our own. Prepare for an assault. We're going in."

CHAPTER SIX

Our Dangerous Mission into the Garden

Pretty scary, huh? You bet it was. But our situation grew even more serious. At that very moment, Drover dropped to the ground like a rock. PLOP! I rushed to his side.

"Dog down, dog down! What happened, son? Can you speak? Are you badly hurt? Can you hear me?"

"Ohhhh! It must have been . . . a ray gun, some kind of deadly ray! He got me. I saw it coming, but I couldn't move out of the way."

"Holy smokes! Does it hurt?"

"Oh yeah, terrible pain."

"Where? Where's the pain?"

51

"Oh, here and here and here, but mostly it's my leg."

"The good one or the bad one?"

"The bad one, and now it's even worse. I don't think I can walk."

"How about crawling? Can you crawl?"

"Nope. Too much pain. I think I'm paralyzed. Oh my leg!"

My mind was swirling. "Okay, trooper, listen carefully. I'll have to go in without you."

"Oh drat! I'm not sure I can live with the guilt!"

"Listen, Drover, this will be hard on you, but you must be brave. I know that you would never fake an injury at a time like this."

There was a moment of silence. "What makes you think that?"

"Well . . . I'm confident that you wouldn't do such a despicable thing. I mean, what kind of dog would fake an injury and leave his partner all alone on the field of combat?"

He let out a moan. "I guess you're right. Yeah, it's real. I'd never play possum on the job."

"See? I knew it. It's bad luck that you took a hit before the action started, and it's badder luck that you'll have to sit this one out."

"Oh the guilt!"

"But you can't go on blaming yourself. You must try to overcome the guilt."

"Ohhh! Well, I guess I can try."

"That's the spirit. Now, sit up and repeat these words: 'It's not my fault and I must live with the guilt.'"

"Well . . . okay, if you think it'll help." He pushed himself up to a sitting position. "It's not my fault and I must . . ."

I stuck my nose in his face and gave him a growl. "Just as I thought, you little faker. You're not hurt, you're not paralyzed, and you're not going to sit this one out."

"Yeah, but . . . help!"

"On your feet, soldier, we're going into combat. Lock and load!"

Drover moaned and whined, but I didn't listen. Can you believe he'd try that stunt on me? The little dunce. Didn't he know I'd seen all his tricks before? Ha.

It was pretty clever, the way I smoked him out, don't you think? You bet.

Our column moved stealthily and stalkingly through the darkness, until we came to the hole under the fence. There, I called a halt and passed on the orders with hand signals. We would dive into the hole and burrow through to the other side. And Drover would go first.

Oh, he moaned and cried over that, but my heart had grown as cold as a block of ice. See, I had every reason to suppose that if I went first, Drover would highball it straight to the machine shed, where he would cower in the shadows until daylight.

He crept into the hole, then stopped. "Hank, it's awfully dark in here."

"What did you expect? Turn on the lights. Hurry up."

"There aren't any lights and . . . what if that thing eats me?"

"You'll get a special award for bravery, and he'll get indigestion. Hurry up!"

At last the little slacker wiggled his way into the garden. I dived into the hole and . . . hmmm, found that it was too small for my enormous body. I crawled out and launched myself into a furious digging procedure, and we're talking about claws that were throwing up boulders and huge gobs of dirt.

Drover waited on the other side, his teeth clacking in fear. "Hank, hurry up! I can see that thing and . . . he looks hungry."

"Drover, I'm digging as fast as I can. If you get impatient, just go whip him yourself."

"I think I'll pass on that. But maybe you could just . . . jump over the fence."

"What? I can't hear you over the roar of all this machinery."

"I said . . . jump the fence! It might be quicker."

Suddenly, a new plan leaped into my mind. I backed my digging equipment out of the hole and shook the dirt off my coat. "Drover, this is taking too long. I'm going to revise our strategy and try to jump the fence."

"Gosh, I never would have thought of that."

"Stand back, son, here come the Marines!"

I loosened up the enormous jumping muscles in my shoulders and hind legs, went into the Deep Crouch Position, and launched myself into the air. Boy, you should have seen it. I cleared the top wire by a good six inches and executed a smooth . . .

Tomato plants? I executed a smooth landing in the middle of some of the . . . uh . . . tomato plants Sally May had set out only days before, but I knew she would understand. In serious combat situations, we expect a few casualties in the . . . uh . . . tomato department, so it was no big deal, no tragedy, nothing we hadn't factored into our . . .

Three tomato plants. Broke 'em smooth off.

Well, that was sad, but we had work to do. Drover's squad and my squad found each other in the darkness and we prepared for the next action. "All right, men, here's the plan. I'll go in the first wave and jump him. When I get him down, you launch the second wave and come in with teeth flashing. This will be a silent run. No barking. We don't want to awaken the house unless it's absolutely necessary."

"I'm too scared to bark anyway."

"What?"

"I said . . . oh boy, combat. Oh goodie."

I placed a paw on his shoulder. "That's the spirit. You know, son, I'm proud of you. If it should happen that one of us doesn't come back from this mission, I just want you to know that . . . well, it's been a real honor serving with you, and if you try to run off, you little weenie, I'll . . . I don't know what I'll do, but you won't like it."

"Gosh. Thanks."

"Let's move out."

It was kind of a touching moment, the Elite Troops of the Security Division saying good-bye on the eve of the dawn of the . . . right before a bloody battle, let us say. And with those last touching words, we turned to the grim task ahead of us.

Was I scared? Nervous? Uneasy? Might as well go ahead and admit it. I mean, who wouldn't have been uneasy? Think about it. We were about to go into deadly combat with a kind of creature we'd never seen before, some kind of robot device that might have come from another solar system or even another galaxy.

We had no blueprints or contagency plans for such creatures. Did they have poison stingers or death rays? Were they protected by some mysterious force field that could deflect our best weapons? We just didn't know, and by the time we had answers to our many questions, it would be . . . well, too late.

So, yes, I felt . . . a little uneasy about this.

On the other hand, protecting the ranch was my job. I had spent my whole life preparing for deadly and dangerous situations. We go into battle, armed with our training, iron discipline, and a special devotion to duty. We give it our best shot. Some of us live to tell about it and to fight another day, and some of us don't.

It's all part of being a cowdog.

Do you feel better now? I don't, because I know what's coming. I mean, all that stuff I said about devotion to duty and so forth was true, but you have NO IDEA what we were fixing to walk into.

And come to think of it . . . are you sure you want to go on with this? I mean, you've had no training in Robot Monsters or Alien Space Devices or stuff like that. What if we get into the middle of the battle and you can't handle it?

Think about it. We could leave this story where it is and switch to another one. How about a nice little story involving . . . well, Little Alfred? Or the cat? Remember Pete? He's a pain in the neck, but there's nothing scary about him.

We could switch stories and we wouldn't have to tell anyone. They'd never know that we . . . well, that we chickened out in the middle of a scary story.

What do you say?

You want to plunge on into the battle?

Okay, it was your decision. I'm ready if you are. Take a deep seat. *We're going in!*

CHAPTER SEVEN

We Engage
the Enemy

Are you still with me? Thanks. I appreciate this, no kidding.

I crept foward through the eerie darkness of night. I could hear my heart thumping. I could hear every breath of air hissing through my nostrils. I could hear the squish and snap of ... well, of tender young tomato plants and pepper plants, as our tanks and armored vehicles bulled their way through the garden.

Thirty seconds into the mission, I switched our sensing devices over to Infra Red. I'm not at liberty to reveal much about those devices, only that we save them for very dangerous missions on very dark nights. They enable us to ...

Sorry, that's all I can say.

Forty-three seconds into the mission I established visual contact with the . . . whatever it was. The Thing, the alien device. I came to a sudden stop, and right then, in that very moment, *I knew something was wrong.*

Did you pick up the clue? Here's the clue. I came to a sudden stop . . . and Drover didn't run into me! I whirled around and saw . . . nothing. Baker Company had left the field of battle. Drover had . . . the little chicken liver! He would pay for this, and I mean, he would pay a terrible price.

Would I abort the mission? No, I had to engage the enemy and go on without backup or support.

I aimed my scanning devices toward the Thing. A glance at the huge screen of my mind showed the same details we had noticed before: long sharp nose, beady little . . . so forth. In other words, the creature hadn't morphed into something bigger or more terrifying.

I took one last gulp of air. In that instant before we launched all dogs, I noticed an important detail: he/it/she/whatever wasn't very big, not much bigger than a cat. If he didn't pull out some kind of deadly secret weapon, maybe, just maybe, I could whip him.

I took one last gulp of . . . I've already said that. The moment of truth had arrived. I threw two switches that armed The Weapon (me), took one last last gulp of air, and hit the GO button.

"Charge! Banzai!"

I had expected our attack to be met by a withering barrage of . . . something. Teeth, claws, snarls, screams, laser weapons, bombs . . . Didn't happen. What happened was that I landed right in the middle of the thing and . . . well, bounced off. My enormous jaws and teeth struck the target dead center, but had no effect. No penetration, no blood, no screams of pain.

Remember our reports about the armored plating? Well, he had armored plating, all right, solid steel two or three inches thick. I might as well have tried to bite a bulldozer.

But here's the rest of it. Once I made contact with the thing, he/it uttered an odd clicking sound and jumped three feet straight up into the air! No kidding, I'd never seen anything that could jump like that. He must have had some kind of high-tech springs on his legs.

Well, our first-wave attack had been replussed . . . repruned . . . repulsed, there we go . . . our first-wave so forth had been repulsed, and the enemy was now hopping around the garden like an . . . I don't know what. Like a jumping bean. Like a pogo stick.

A lot of dogs would have shut 'er down right

there and gone back to the office. Not me, fellers. I was more determined than ever to get a good bite on this guy and give him the thrashing he so richly deserved.

You know why? Cowdog Pride. Devotion to duty. A sense of higher purpose. Also, heh heh, I had made a very interesting discovery: this guy didn't bite, kick, claw, or even hiss. All he did was make that clicking noise and hop around. He was a villain, but a cowardly villain.

In other words, this was the kind of fight every dog dreams of! Lots of action, but no great shedding of blood.

Yes sir, and with Cowdog Pride shining forth in the depths of my soul, I launched another attack at the little ... CLUNK ... the steel plating rattled my jaws a bit, but I'm no quitter. I launched another ... CLUNK ... and chased the little coward around and around the garden.

He thought he could get away from me? Outrun or outlast the Head of Ranch Security? Ha! Little did he know. This guy was fixing to learn a lesson or two about ...

HUH?

I couldn't believe it.

You won't believe it either.

Get this. One second he was there in front of

me, and the next second he had . . . *vanished into the earth*! No kidding. I mean, it was as though a hole had opened up in the ground and he'd dived into it.

But wait. There was more to this than you might have supposed. That hole in the earth didn't just open up by itself. The creature had dug his own hole and had burrowed into the ground . . . before my very eyes, while I was standing there watching!

Impossible. Our department had files and reports on every kind of animal known to inhabit the ranch. Our flies contained nothing . . . our *files*, let us say, contained nothing to suggest the existence of an armor-plated animal that could dig itself a hole in a matter of seconds. And that's when I knew for certain that this was no earthly animal.

I had suspected it from the very beginning, and now I had irreguffable proof. Our forces had come face-to-face with some kind of robot device from another galaxy, an unmanned space probe that had the ability to burrow into the ground and hide beneath the planetary surface.

Pretty shocking, huh? You bet. And now you know why we named this case "The Burrowing Robot." Because it *was* a burrowing robot.

Well, there I stood, all alone in the garden.

Drover had vanished and so had the enemy space probe. I could hear the Thing digging underground, and every now and then it transmitted that same clicking sound—no doubt some kind of coded radio signal, beamed back to its home planet.

What was I supposed to do now? Nothing in all my years of training had prepared me for this moment. Should I retire from the field of battle, go back to the office, and try to forget the whole episode? Most dogs would have done that, you know, and wouldn't have spent even a second worrying about it.

Me? I worried about such things, and for good reason. Consider this. That thing was sending signals back to its home planet, right? Well, what if the signals got through? And what if they sent a whole army of invading robots back to save the first one? Then, instead of having one space probe robot burrowed in the garden, we might have fifty or a hundred of the things running around the ranch. And digging holes.

On the other hand . . . maybe I could dig him out. I mean, I was a pretty awesome digger. I had proved that on many occasions. If I couldn't actually cause him any bodily harm (the steel plating), at least I could run him out of Sally May's garden and teach him a lesson.

But, of course, in order to do that, I would have to ... uh ... do some pretty radical dirt moving in ... uh ... the very garden I was trying to protect. And you might remember what Slim and Sally May had said about that.

It was one of the most difficult moral decisions I had faced in my whole career. I felt the terrible burden of responsibility that came with the job, and all at once I found myself ... well, chewing my paw.

Does that strike you as odd? Well, it's not. In fact, it's the kind of response any normal, healthy American dog would have made in such a time of crisis. When we face unbearable moral decisions, when we feel ourselves being crushed by the responsibility of running our ranches, we often ... well ... chew our paws.

Why? I'm not sure. Maybe it appears irrational and silly, but it makes us feel better. And besides, there was nobody around to see me doing it.

I was in the process of chewing my left paw and mulling over the crushing so forth of the so forth, when I heard a sound to my left. Was that some kind of clue? I was chewing my *left* paw and I had heard a sound to my ... no, it wasn't a clue. It was ...

... a cat.

Pete. Have we discussed Pete? Maybe not, so let's get it over with. Pete was our local cat. I had no use for cats in general, and I had even less use for Pete, who was snotty, arrogant, dishonest, lazy, and dumb beyond belief.

And you know what else? The little pest had a genius for showing up at just the wrong moments. Yes, I'm aware that *dumb* and *genius* don't exactly fit together, but somehow they both occured every time this sniveling, scheming little freeloader of a cat showed up.

And there he was, purring and rubbing his way down the garden fence—at the very moment when I needed time alone to ponder my heavy decision and . . . well, chew my paw.

I heard his whiny voice. "Mmmmm, hello, Hankie. Out for a little stroll in the garden?"

"Kitty, let me go straight to the point. There's never a good time for you to walk into my life, but this time is even worse than most. I'm very busy right now."

"Mmm, yes, I can tell. You're . . . well, you seem to be . . . chewing your paw."

"That's what you think I'm doing, Pete, but the truth is much deeper than that. You wouldn't understand, so I won't bother to explain."

In the moonlight, I could see him grinning at

me with that . . . that smirk that drives me nuts. "You know, Hankie, I don't know why I'm telling you this, but I might be able to help."

That brought forth a rumble of laughter. "You? Help me? Ha ha! That's the dumbest thing you've ever said, Pete, and you hold the record for dumb remarks. In the first place, I don't need help. In the second place, if I needed help, you'd be the last one I'd call. And in the third place . . . what exactly did you mean by that?"

"Well, Hankie, I can tell you what's in the hole."

Well, he wasn't going to take a hint and go away. That was no surprise. Cats never take hints. I heaved a sigh, marched over to the fence, and beamed a glare at the grinning cat.

"Have you been spying on me again? How did you know there was something in the hole?"

"Well, I was watching, Hankie. We cats are very observant, you know. Very little goes on around here that I don't notice, especially at night."

"Oh yeah?"

"Mm hmm. I saw it all, Hankie, and I can tell you what that thing was."

"For your information, Kitty, I've been working this case for the past hour, and I know exactly what it was. I don't need a shrimpy little cat to tell me what I've seen with my own eyes, and even if a shrimpy little cat had an opinion, I wouldn't believe it. But just for laughs, what's your point?"

Pete flopped over on his back and rolled around in the dirt. "It begins with an A and ends with an O."

"That's rubbish, Pete. You don't know what you're . . ."

"The second letter is an R, and the third letter is an M."

"A-R-M, with an O at the end? Armo?" I couldn't hold back my laughter. "Ha ha ha. Not even close, Kitty, sorry, and I'm afraid we're out of time." I lowered my nose and narrowed my eyes. "You want to know what's in the hole? Okay, I'll tell you, but you have to promise to scram and leave me in peace. For your information, the object in the hole is a Burrowing Robot from another planet."

For some reason, the cat . . . the dumb cat broke into gales of laughter, and as he staggered away from the garden, laughing his stupid head off, he said, "You're right, Hankie! That's just what it was! Ho ho! A Burrowing Robot! Hee hee!"

CHAPTER EIGHT

We Come Under Heavy Fire

I must admit that something troubled me about the cat's weird behavior. For one thing, he'd broken into a fit of hysterical laughter. As a general rule, cats have no sense of humor, so when they start laughing for no apparent reason . . . well, it makes a guy wonder.

Then there was a tiny detail you probably didn't pick it up. *Pete had admitted that I was right.* Now, that was really strange. See, cats are so haughty and arrogant, they can never bring themselves to admit that anyone else in the world, and especially a dog, might be right about anything. Yet Pete had said . . . hmmmm.

And then there was a third matter that caused me the greatest concern of all. *Cats lie.* They lie all the time. They tell big whopperous lies, even when it would be easier to tell the truth. No one should ever trust a cat or believe anything a cat says. Hencely, when Pete had admitted that I was right . . . phooey.

It was too complicated. I had more important things to do with my life than to make sense out of a cat's nonsense. I whirled away from the fence and marched back to . . .

A word that began with an A and ended with an O?

. . . and marched straight back to the hole in the earthly dirt of the garden.

The first three letters were A-R-M? Hmmm.

And there, I put all thoughts of cats and so-called armos out of my mind and concentrated on the difficult decision that lay before me: would I start digging and . . .

Armarillo? Armaretto?

. . . would I start digging and try to flush the mysterious space device out of its hole, or would I admit defeat and go back to bed?

Armamento?

But the important thing was that I totally ignored and forgot my wasted conversation with the . . .

Armadiggo?

. . . with the scheming, cheating, troublemaking cat, and got back to the important tasks at hand.

Where was I? Oh yes, chewing my paw. I sat down beside the hole in the garden and gnawed my foot and directed all my powers of concentration on the huge moral dilemmon that faced me. I tried to imagine what Sally May would want me to do in this situation—accept a shameful defeat, or throw the rascal out of her garden?

All at once the decision seemed easy. I mean, when I framed it up from Sally May's point of view, it seemed clear and obvious that she would want me to finish the job I had started and free her precious garden of all robots and space probes.

If I happened to . . . well, enlarge the hole somewhat and destroy a few rows of tomato plants, she would understand that I was doing it all . . . *for her*. In fact, I could almost hear her voice, cheering me on to victory: "You go get him, Hank! We're just lucky we have a dog on the ranch who really cares about protecting the garden!"

Well, what could I say? If Sally May wanted me to finish the job, by George I would finish the job.

With a vision of her sweet smiling face glowing in the afterburners of my mind, I plunged into the task with a kind of fury unknown to ordinary dogs. For Sally May, I would give my last ounce of energy to the task, and my very life if necessary. Anything and everything for Sally May!

Fellers, you should have seen me. I attacked the hole and became a huge trenching machine, a whirling buzzsaw of paws and claws. Within mere seconds . . . okay, within mere minutes . . . quite a few minutes later . . . it took me a while, but within half an hour or so I had moved enough dirt out of the hole to expose the invader.

Yes, there he was, and I could hear my claws scraping across the steel plating of his armor. It appeared that I had him this time, but then . . .

HUH?

I was a pretty awesome digger, but that guy could dig like nothing I'd ever seen before! Just when I thought I had him in the grisp of my grasp, he . . . well, dug deeper. And made that same clicking noise.

At last, exhausted and heaving for breath, I backed out of the hole and did a thorough review of my battle plan. Okay, maybe I couldn't actually dig him out, but I could sure as heck put out the call for fresh troops. I would alert the house and someone, probably Loper, would come rushing down to help. He would fetch a shovel from the shed and together we would finish the job.

After renewing my body's vital supply of carbon

diego, I launched a major Barking Offensive. This wasn't some measly bark-at-the-coyotes kind of deal, or a barking routine I might use to humble the cat. No sir. This was a full-blown Alert and Alarm.

I heard the door open up at the house. "Hank, shut up that barking!"

Huh? Shut up that . . . hey, we had a Code Three Situtation in the garden area! Maybe Loper thought I was just . . . well, barking, so I barked even houder and larder . . . louder and harder, let us say, to let him know that I wasn't kidding this time.

"Hank! One more time, buddy!"

He wanted me to bark one more time? Sure, you bet, I could handle that. I barked one more time, and then ten more times just for good . . .

BAM!

Suddenly I heard the, uh, roar of a shotgun and the whistling of something overhead, which might very well have been . . . buckshot.

"Now, shut up and let us get some dadgum sleep!"

The door slammed. A deadly silence moved over the garden area. Okay, fine. I could stop barking. I could shut up, if that's . . . sometimes these humans don't seem totally rational, especially at night. I mean, we dogs are out there in the darkness, try-ing to protect the ranch from all kinds of things, and the people show no appreciation at all.

None. Zero. Instead of showing appreciation, they screech and bellow and fire guns at the very dogs who . . . I've said this before, but it bears repeating: in some ways, this is a LOUSY JOB.

Oh well.

And by the way, I said that "a deadly silence" moved over the garden, remember? Well, it turned out to be not so silent, because I could still hear that mysterious clicking sound coming from inside the hole.

The Burrowing Robot was still trying to beam a message back to his home planet.

So what was I supposed to do, sit there and say "duhhhh" while he called in a whole army of space invaders? Heck no, not me. The House Crowd had shut down my barking attack, but nobody had said anything about digging. By George, I would dig all night, and when the humans came out of the house in the morning, I would have something to show them.

And then, wouldn't they feel foolish and sorry for screeching and firing cannons at their Head of Ranch Security? Yes, they would.

I was about to go back into the hole, when I heard a voice: "Hank, what are you doing in there? Hank? Can you hear me?"

I marched over to the north side of the garden fence and beamed a blistering glare at . . . did you guess who it was?

"Drover, I have very few words to say to you."

"Oh, good. I thought you'd be . . . well, a little mad."

"Oh no, I'm not a little mad. I'm a whole bunch mad! And do you know why?"

He hung his head. "Well . . . 'cause I ran away? 'Cause I'm scared of things in the dark?"

"Yes, exactly, which proves that you knew what you were doing. You left a superior officer on the field of battle, to be mauled by some Creature of the Night."

"Yeah, but . . . you didn't get mauled. But you do have a mudball on the end of your nose."

I turned away and swiped the . . . it appeared that in the process of digging and so forth, I had acquired a, uh, muddish protuberance on the end of my, uh, nose, so to speak. I brushed it off and turned my flaming eyes back on the little wretch.

"For leaving the field of battle, you get five Chicken Marks."

"Oh drat."

"Six. One for using naughty language at the scene of a crime."

"Oh good."

"Seven Chicken Marks! One more for not being properly chastened."

"Yeah, but I wasn't chasin'. You were."

"Don't try to be funny, Drover. I'm in no mood for that."

"But you know what? I just figured out what that thing was you were chasing."

"Drover, I've been working this case all night. I've engaged him in hand-to-hand combat several times. I know what I've been chasing."

"Yeah, and it wasn't a robot. It's an animal that lives in South Texas, has a shell on his body, it's called . . . oh fiddle, I can't remember the name."

I studied the runt. In the pale light of the moon, he had the look of a moron. I decided to run a little test on him. "Does it begin with an A?"

"An A. Let me think." He rolled his eyes around and squeezed his lisp together . . . his lips, that is. "You know, I think it does start with an A."

"And the second letter is an R?" He grinned and nodded. "And the third letter is an M?"

He started hopping up and down. "A-R-M . . . yeah, I think that's it! Keep going. What's the rest of it?"

I stuck my nose into his face. "The rest of it is that you've been talking to the cat. I don't know what you guys are trying to pull, Drover, but I must warn you that associating with cats is strictly against regulations."

"Yeah, but I haven't seen Pete all night."

"Don't argue with me. Pete's trying to pull some kind of scam on me, and somehow you got sucked into it."

"I did?"

"Yes, you did. Now, get yourself back in this garden and lend a hand. We've got a deadly Burrowing Robot trapped in a hole, and we're fixing to dig him out."

Drover's ears jumped up. "Deadly? You really think he's . . . deadly?"

"We have to assume that, son. With these space devices . . . why are you backing away?"

"Well, it's these allergies. Achoo! Achoo! All ad wudst, by dose is all stobbed ub."

"Come back here, you little . . . Drover, I'm ordering you . . . !"

"Achoo! Achoo! Better go, Hank. Sorry. I feel terrible about this. Bye now."

And with that, he vanished into the night. "All right, go ahead, run away! You'll pay a terrible price for this! Ten Chicken Marks!"

Off in the distance, I heard him yell, "Oh my leg! Oh by doze!"

The little faker. The little weenie. Imagine, him

and the cat trying to pull some kind of wool over my ice. Ha. Oh well, I'd be better off without him.

I returned to the excavation site. For a moment, I stood still and listened. Yes, there it was again, the same clicking sound, coming from underground. The device was still transmitting.

I took a huge gulp of air and loosened up my enormous muscles. I had to . . . yawn . . . dig him out. There was no other . . . yawn . . . solution to the . . . yawn . . . all at once, I felt kind of tired. Weary. Worn down to a shallow of my former shelf.

Maybe . . . just a quick nap. Nothing major, just a few winks to . . .

PLUNK!

Zzzzzzzzzzzzzzzzzzzzzzzzzzzzzzzzzzzzzzzzzzzzzzzz

CHAPTER NINE

Tragedy
and Failure

Maybe my body was more exhausted than I'd thought. I mean, how else can you explain that I collapsed on the ground and fell instantly to sleep?

Sheer exhaustion. Overwork. Tension, nerves, the crushing responsibility of . . .

HUH?

I lifted my head. My eyes slid open, rolled around three times, and came into focus. The sun was up. The birds were chirping. Three huge humanoid creatures towered above me. They looked . . . well, shocked and astammered, and maybe even . . . mad.

Yes, mad. They all looked mad.

The female humanoid slapped her forehead

with the palm of her hand and screeched, "Oh, for crying in the bucket! Hank . . . look what you've done to my garden!!"

HUH?

Garden? I let my eyes drift around the . . . well, the immediate vicinity and . . . sure enough, I was lying in . . . uh . . . someone's garden, it appeared. On top of a rather large pile of . . . uh . . . fresh dirt, so to speak. And several feet away was a . . . well, a pretty big hole in the . . . uh . . . ground.

And suddenly it all came rushing back. I was in Sally May's garden, and she was the female humanoid who had . . .

Uh-oh.

Slowly and quietly, I reached for the control panel and threw a switch marked *"Oops."* This activated a program we use only in the darkest and direst of emergency situations. Oops is similar to The Sharing of Pain, only when we activate Oops, the pain is on the other foot, so to speak.

I was in deep trouble, fellers. I knew it. I could see it in their eyes. And I had to admit that the evidence looked pretty . . . oh brother, I was cooked!

The Oops Program kicked in. Within seconds, my tail began tapping out a slow, sad rhythm, and we're talking about the saddest rhythm you can imagine. Pure tragedy. My eyes glazed over and locked into the setting we call Deepest Remorse. And whilst all that was going on, the facial muscles in my face began beaming a message of earnest sincerity:

"Sally May, I know this looks bad. I know our relationship hasn't flown like a straight arrow into the bull's-eye of Happiness. I know how you feel about your . . . uh . . . garden, but if you'll just give me a minute or . . . maybe an hour, I can explain

everything. See, there's a Burrowing Robot space device in that hole. No kidding. I've been working this case all night. I've been doing it . . . *for you*."

The silence was poisonous. Would it sell? I held my breath and waited for Oops to do its work.

My eyes flicked from one face to the other. Loper's looked like the face of a two-thousand-year-old mummy. Slim's reminded me of petrified wood. And Sally May's face . . . yipes. She covered it with her hands and moaned, "All that work!"

And with that, they walked out of the garden, all three of them. Sally May was leaning on her husband's shoulder, like a woman in grief. Slim and Loper walked with their heads bowed. Nobody said another word, and I was left just . . . sitting there.

What was this? I mean, why didn't they yell and scream, call me names, jump up and down, bellow, throw clods, threaten and sputter, bulge out their eyeballs and blood vessels, screech, stomp on their hats, chase me around with the broom?

That's the way we'd always done it before, back in the Good Old Days. That's the kind of response I expected and could relate to. But . . . this . . . this Silent Treatment!

I didn't know what to do or how to respond. Well, yes I did. I seized the microphone. "Control, this is Leper Colony. Your Oops Program stinks. I don't know what you guys do in there, but you've just ruined my life!"

I held my breath and waited for a reply. Seconds later, a message flashed across the screen of my mind. *"The answer to the Riddle of Life is: Potato Soup."*

Great.

I pushed myself up on all fours and started . . . clicking? That same clicking noise, coming from the dark depths of the ground? The robot device was still in there, and still transmitting, but it no longer mattered. I no longer cared.

Their Silent Rebukes had wounded me more deeply than sticks and stones, slings and arrows, or swords of sharpened steel. If only they had screamed at me, maybe I could have bounced back and recovered some of my spiritual whatever, but their silence . . . their cold, rebuking silence had ripped my spirit like a pair of old jeans on a fat man who bends over to pick up a comb that has fallen out of his shirt pocket.

Their Silent Rebukes had ripped me . . . bad. Broken my spirit. Broken my heart. Left me feeling like a louse and a rat, and like a rat covered with louses. Lice.

I no longer cared about the Burrowing Robot.

I didn't care if he called in an invasion of space monsters. I didn't care about me or the ranch or anything. Nothing mattered anymore.

With my head hanging so low that my nose clipped the tops of several dirt piles, I trudged out of the garden. My tail had become a lifeless column of bone and flesh, something dead that followed me around, like a piece of limp rubber garden hose on a hot summer day.

I knew what lay ahead of me now. I had no choice. My career on the ranch was finished. I would have to resign in disgrace, leave the ranch forever, and take up a new existence as a hollow soul in the wilderness. A dog without a home, a dog without a country.

As I trudged out the garden gate, I came face-to-face with the same goldbricking little tunafish who had abandoned me in the night. Drover.

He gave me a nervous grin. "Did you get in trouble?"

"What do you think?"

"I think . . . maybe you did. But you know what? I just remembered the name of that thing in the hole. It's an . . ."

"Save it for someone who cares, Drover. That's not me. I'm resigning my position as Head of Ranch Security."

He stared at me and gasped. "Resigning . . . yeah but . . . you can't . . . oh my gosh! You mean . . ."

"Yes, Drover, I'm leaving this hateful place. I tried to care, I tried to do my job, but it has all ended in shame and disgrace. Step aside or I'll have to walk over your face."

He stepped aside and started following me. "Hank, wait, you can't do this to me! If you leave . . . oh my gosh, who'll take care of the ranch?"

"You or Pete, J. T. Cluck, a committee of chickens, the coyotes. I don't care, Drover. It's your problem now."

"Yeah but . . . where will you go? What'll you do?"

"I'm going to the wilderness, of course. That's where dogs go when they've fallen into disgrace and disrepair."

"Yeah but . . . what'll you eat?"

"Grub worms. Grasshoppers. Roots and berries. To tell you the truth, Drover, I don't know what I'll eat. Maybe I won't eat anything. Maybe I'll *be* eaten by coyotes or savage monsters. A guy never knows what might happen when he's driven into exile."

"Oh my gosh, don't even say that!"

"Why? If I got eaten by cannibals, I'm sure Sally May would be happy. I've spent my whole life trying to please that woman, and feeding myself to the cannibals is the only thing I haven't tried. Who knows, it might work."

The little mutt was almost in tears. "Listen, Hank, maybe you can patch things up, and . . . and I'll help."

"You'll help? Ha ha. What a pathetic joke. Drover, when you show up to help, it's like three good dogs just walked off the job. No thanks."

He fell to the ground and began kicking his legs in the air. "It's all my fault! I'm such a failure! Oh, my leg! Oh, the guilt!"

"Good-bye, Drover. I hope you take good care of the ranch—although at a deeper level, I really don't give a rip. See you around."

And with that, I left Drover and marched away from the ranch I had loved and protected for so many years. Drover tried to call me back, but my heart had turned to stone. On and on I marched, holding my head as high as I . . .

I whirled around and marched back to him. "Drover, one last desperate thought. You mentioned something about a name."

He peeked out at me through his paws, which were covering his eyes. "I did?"

"Yes, you did, the name of that creature in the hole. What was that all about? If, by some miracle, you could bring some new information to this case . . . well, it might help."

He uncovered his eyes and rolled them around. "Oh yeah, I did."

"Yes? Well? Go on, out with it."

"Let me think here. It was a . . . it was a . . ." He burst out crying. "I can't remember! You've got me so upset, I can't remember my own name!"

The air hissed out of my lungs. "Your name is Drover."

"No, I think it's Rupert."

"Rupert was your pet bone. Don't you remember?"

"No, I think his name was . . . Armadillo."

"Armadillo? What a silly name for a friend."

"Well, he was only a bone."

"Good point, but you know what? I still don't care. Good-bye, Drupert, and this time it's forever."

"Hey, wait! I just remembered. My name's Drover, just plain old Drover."

"Please don't ever speak to me again."

"Oh my leg! Oh the guilt! Help, murder!"

I left him there, squawking and rolling around in the dirt, and pointed myself toward the wilderness.

Where, exactly, was the wilderness? Well, it began about a hundred yards south of headquarters. It included all parts of the ranch where we dogs seldom ventured, and to be honest, it was kind of a . . . gulp . . . scary place.

I mean, there was an invisible line that separated our headquarters compound from the rest of the universe, and we dogs spent most of our time inside that line. What lay outside was . . . well, an unchartered wilderness. The Great Unknown. It was a place inhabited by . . . gulp . . . savage coyotes, bobcats, monsters, hissing snakes . . .

Have we discussed hissing snakes? I don't get along with hissing snakes, even those that don't hiss. I mean, your bullsnakes and your garter snakes are fairly harmless, but they're very creepy and I don't like 'em at all. And your rattlesnakes . . .

I, uh, halted my march on the edge of the Wilderness Line and looked back toward headquarters. I mean, there was always a chance that Sally May might have seen me leaving and would come . . . well, rushing out of the house to call me back . . . to tell me, through her tears, that she was sorry for everything and that we should try to patch up our relationship one last time.

A guy should never give up hope, right?

I waited and watched. Sally May didn't come rushing out of the . . . okay, maybe Little Alfred would try to call me back. Surely he would notice the huge void that opened up the moment I walked away from the ranch, I mean, "a boy and his dog" and all of that.

I waited and watched. Little Alfred didn't come.

Okay, maybe Slim. Slim and I had been the best of pals for many years, why, we'd even shared sandwiches together, and beef jerky. I'd slept in his bed, drunk water out of his commode, ridden hundreds of miles with him in the pickup. Ours was a relationship that could withstand the storms of Life's . . .

Nobody came. I couldn't believe it. *What was wrong with those people!* There I was, giving them one last chance to beg me back to the ranch and they were throwing it all away?

Gulp.

I turned south and marched into my Wilderness Exile.

CHAPTER TEN

The Wilderness
Exile Begins

I knew right away that I wasn't going to enjoy my exile experience. Once I had dropped over the horizon and had left cizivilation behind me . . . cizilivation . . . civilization behind me, I began to notice . . . well, all kinds of creepy things I'd never noticed before.

You know that juniper tree on the south side of the creek? Back in happier times, I had marked it several times for communication purposes, and it had always struck me as a happy little evergreen tree. But now? It didn't look happy. In fact, it seemed to have taken on the shape of a . . . well, some kind of headless phantom . . . wrapped in a cape.

And you know those big cottonwood trees down by the creek? I'd always thought of cottonwoods as big friendly trees, trees that offered shade on a hot summer day, trees that welcomed a weary traveler.

All at once they didn't look so friendly. They looked old and gnarled, stern and angry, and their outstretched limbs reminded me of . . . well, claws.

And remember those willow trees that grew down in the creek bottom? All at once I recalled another name for a willow tree: *weeping willow*. Why? I have no idea, but all of a sudden the name sort of fit, I mean, those willows looked very sad about something and even made a moaning sound in the wind.

As you can see, my exile had gotten off to a bad start. Five minutes alone in the wilderness might have been fun, but the rest of my life?

Gulp.

You might say that I didn't do much of anything for the rest of the day. I just wandered around in circles, trying to avoid monsters and hoping that someone up at the house would . . .

But then the sun went down, and long shadows started creeping across the land, and things got ten times worse. Night birds made eerie sounds. Distant coyotes shrieked and cackled. Bats zipped past, little winged phantoms that never gave you time to see them. Every bush became a slouching monster, every tree a skeleton's bony hand, every shadow a . . .

I was huddled in some weeds, peering out at this endless parade of nightmares, when my keen eyes picked up a blur of motion in the distance. At first I thought my imagination was playing tricks on me, but then . . . there it was again.

Something moved, about twenty-five yards to the east.

I raised my head above the weed tops and studied the spot. It appeared to be . . . a bird of some kind, larger than your sparrows and larks, but smaller than your turkeys and buzzards. Yes, it was a bird, and it seemed to be . . . hmm, how odd.

This bird seemed to be running around with its wings outstretched, making some kind of weird noise: "Vrrrrrrroom! Vrrrroooom!" What was this? I raised myself higher out of the weeds and took a closer look.

It was a bird all right, perhaps one of the varieties of owl that inhabit our ranch. We have several kinds of owl, you know: your great horned owl, your barn owl, your burrowing owl, your . . .

It was a burrowing owl, no question about it. They're quite a bit smaller than your other owls, and they spend a lot of time on the ground. Your other varieties of owl don't walk or run. They fly. This one appeared to be . . . well, running around and making that peculiar sound—"Vrrrrroooom!"

Oh, and my keen eyes soon picked up another important clue. The alleged owl appeared to be of the female variety, in other words, a woman. A lady owl.

Then it hit me like a load of hay falling off the Truck of Life. I *knew* that owl!

"Hey, Madame? Madame Moonshine, the witchy little owl? Is that you out there?"

She stopped in her tracks. Still holding her wings out to the sides, she rolled her head around in my direction. "Sorry, I'm not home. You'll have to try later. Vrrrroooom!"

She was off again, swooping in circles beneath the cottonwood trees. Pretty odd behavior, don't you think? I thought so, but that was no huge surprise. I mean, I'd had some dealings with Madame Moonshine before, and I'd always found her a little . . . well, odd. Strange.

But you know what else? Madame Moonshine had special powers. She saw things others couldn't see, and could do things others couldn't do. On several occasions in the past, I had gone to her with special problems, and she'd always been able to help. Remember the time I'd come down with Eye-Crosserosis? She'd cured me of that terrible disease, using her special riddles.

And maybe, just maybe, she could help me out of this Exile Problem. It was worth a try.

I pushed myself out of the weeds and walked out into the clearing where she was ... doing whatever she was doing. To be honest, I couldn't make much sense out of it. While I waited to be recognized and spoken to, she swooped in big circles around me.

The minutes dragged on and, well, you know me. I don't enjoy waiting. I get impatient. I'm a very busy dog and don't have time to waste on ... okay, I had all the time in the world, now that I was unemployed, but still ...

"Uh ... Madame? I hate to barge in on you like this, but ..."

"Vrrrrooom! Vrrrrrooom! Cleopatra rode down the Nile in a barge. Take the E out of Nile and it becomes *nil*. Nil is nothing. If it weren't for that one little E, she would have been floating her barge on a river of sheer nothingness! Had you ever thought of that?"

"Uh ... no ma'am, I hadn't thought of that."

"It's something to ponder. Just think of the power: one tiny letter can cause a mighty river to go dry!"

"I'll be derned. Anyway, I was just out for a little stroll and saw you ... uh ... what is it you're doing?"

"Vrrrrooom! Vrrrrroooom! I'm pretending that I'm a bird. I'm spreading my wings, you see, and trying to fly."

"No kidding? At night, in the dark? Gee, what

a . . . what an interesting thing to be doing. But Madame, that noise you're making . . . well, it sounds kind of like a motor."

"You mean . . . vrooom, vrrroom?"

"Yes, right, that's it. Don't you think it sounds like a motor?"

"Of course it does, you ninny! I'm a motorized bird."

"Oh. Ha ha. So you're playing . . . airplane?"

She stopped running and folded up her wings, then came hopping over to me. *Boink, boink.* That's what they do, you know, your burrowing owls. They hop.

She twisted her head and stared at me with her big yellow eyes. "What did you say?"

"I said, you seem to be playing airplane."

"I was *not* playing airplane. I was playing motorized bird."

"Yeah, but what's a motorized bird? It's an airplane, right?"

She sighed and rolled her eyes. "A motorized bird is a bird with a motor. Without the motor it's still a bird but not a motorized bird. I was studying the effects of industrialization on the flight patterns of birds."

"Yeah, but . . . you didn't really have a motor. You were just pretending. All you had was the sound."

She gave me an owlish stare. "Who are you? And what gives you the right to say these outrageous things?"

"Well, ma'am, I'm Hank the Cowdog. We've met, several times, in fact. I'm sure you remember me."

"I don't remember you. Wait. Are you the one who calls himself Hank the Rabbit?"

"Uh . . . no ma'am. For some reason, you've always called me that, but it's not my real name. And I'm not a rabbit."

She glanced over both shoulders. "Something strange is going on here. Do you have an appointment?"

"Not exactly. No. See, I just quit my . . . I'm in a bind, Madame, and I was wondering if you might give me some . . ."

"Never mind. Let's go to my office."

She hopped away, and I followed her. We made our way down the north edge of the creek, until we came to a small cave in the side of the creek bank. As we approached, she called out, "Timothy? Make way! Open the outer doors!"

Now get this. There were no "outer doors" on the cave. It was just an ordinary hole in the ground. The so-called doors consisted of Madame's pet rattlesnake and bodyguard, Big Tim. Remember Big Tim? He was about the biggest, nastiest-looking rattlesnake I'd ever seen, and his looks hadn't improved one bit since the last time we'd met.

Big Tim had been coiled up at the entrance of the cave, and when he heard us coming, he slithered his fat diamondback self over to the side. Madame Moonshine hopped into the cave, and I . . . uh . . . stopped. Big Tim and I exchanged looks. Yipes! Those cold green eyes made the hair stand up on the back of my neck.

"How's it going, Tim? Been busy, I guess, huh?"

He stuck out his forked tongue at me.

"Well, great to see you again. Tell the family hello."

I rushed past him and dived into the hole. There, I found myself wedged inside a narrow passageway that didn't quite fit the shape of my body. I got my head and shoulders into it, but my hinelary region didn't make the squeeze. It appeared that I was hung up and would have to . . .

Outside the hole, I heard Big Tim rattle and hiss. I could almost see him slithering his snakely body into a big nasty coil—and taking aim at my hiney. Suddenly, I felt new reserves of energy coursing through my body. I shifted all four legs into Turbo Dig, bulled my way through the passage, and rolled into the main room of the cave.

There was Madame Moonshine, perched on a

kind of platform at the front, clutching a bone in her left claw. A shaft of silver moonlight beamed through a hole in the roof and fell upon her head, giving her a kind of ghostly appearance. Above her head, exposed tree roots hung from the ceiling—like long skinny fingers . . . or snakes.

She blinked her eyes at me. "Now, tell me again why you're here."

"Well, I . . . I don't think I had a chance to tell you the first time, Madame."

"Ah. So we missed the first time. Let's skip the second time and go to the third. Second times always seem so boring. For the third time, O Rabbity Hank, what brings you to my cave?"

"Well, I was watching you run around in circles, and you were making the sounds of a motorized bird. We talked for a moment, then you invited me in here."

She clapped her wings together. "Yes, of course. It's coming back to me now. You're troubled."

"Yes ma'am, it's true. See, I've had this little . . ."

"Yes indeed, very troubled. I saw it right away. Shall I go on? You must be prepared to accept the truth."

"Well, sure."

"Sit down. The truth always comes as a jolt." I sat down. Madame closed her eyes and waved her wings back and forth. "Yes, I see it clearly. You're very troubled." Her eyes popped open. "You must stop thinking of yourself as a rabbit. You're not a rabbit, nor will you ever be a rabbit."

I stared at her. "Hey, wait a minute. That's not my problem. See, you're the one who calls me Hank the Rabbit."

"And . . . your name *isn't* Hank?"

"No, my name is Hank, but I'm not a rabbit."

"Have you ever wanted to be a rabbit?"

"No ma'am, never."

She scowled. "Hmmmm. Have you ever wanted to be a motorized bird?"

"No ma'am, absolutely not."

Her scowl deepened. "Hmmm. Have you ever *seen* a motorized bird?"

"Well, I . . . not until tonight."

She lifted one wing in the air. "Ah! We've found the source of your problem." She leaned forward and whispered, *"There's no such thing as a motorized bird!* And anyone who thinks he's seen one might very well think he's a rabbit."

The air hissed out of my chest. This wasn't going well.

CHAPTER ELEVEN

Madame Moonshine Works Her Magic

Madame Moonshine blinked her big eyes and smiled. "Well? Do you feel better now?"

"No ma'am, I'm feeling worse."

"It's always difficult to give up our illusions. For years, you've wanted to be a rabbit, a soft, cuddly rabbit with velvety hair. But Hank, that's not you."

"I know."

"You must give it up."

"I've given it up. I never had it."

"Then why," she twisted her head to the side, "have I been calling you Hank the Rabbit all these years?"

"I've wondered that myself, and do you want to hear my theory?"

She yawned. "Is it long and complicated? I missed my nap today."

"No ma'am, it's short and simple."

"Oh, very well. Let's hear your theory."

"My theory, Madame, is that you're just a little bit . . . *weird*. In other words, the problem is you, not me." She had fallen asleep. "Hey! Wake up! You slept through my theory."

She sat up and rubbed her eyes. "Oh dear. How was it?"

"It was great. I said *you're weird*, and that's why you call me Hank the Rabbit."

She smiled, rubbed her wings together, and began hopping around. "Oh Hank, you are clever beyond my wildest expectations! Do you see what you've done?"

"Sure. I told the truth. You're a weird little owl, and I'm sorry to be the one to give you the bad news."

"But it's not bad news, it's wonderful news! Don't you see? You've passed the First Test!"

"Huh? What's the First Test?"

"On the Path to Truth, we must face a series of tests: the first, the third, and the fourth."

"What about the second?"

"You noticed! Oh, you are a clever fellow. We always skip the second step in everything." She flopped down and rested her head on one wing. "Has anyone ever suggested that you might be a genius?"

"Well, I . . . you wouldn't think that I'm bragging?"

"Not at all."

"To be honest, Madame, it's been said that I'm a very intelligent dog, maybe one of the smartest dogs in the whole world. No kidding."

"I knew it, I knew it! Oh, this is marvelous. Are you ready for the Third Test?"

"Sure, I guess so, although I'm starting to wonder . . ."

"Shhhh! Silence. We must have absolute silence while I adminster the Third Test." She leaped to her feet, closed her eyes, and rocked back and forth on her skinny legs. (She had skinny legs. I picked up that clue right away.) "The Third Test will be a song."

"You mean . . . it'll be easy, like a piece of cake?"

"Can you sing a piece of cake?"

"No ma'am, I don't think so."

"Then please hush and listen. The test questions are contained in the song. After the song, I will ask for your answer."

I listened to her song. As you'll see, it was a little . . . I won't say any more about it or give you any hints. You can decide for yourself.

The Song of the Third Test of Truth

How much wood could a woodpecker chuck,
If a peckerwood's a checkerboard square?
How much chuck would a peckerwood peck
If the checkerboard's just thin air?

If the checkerboard's round
And sold by the pound,
Then a woodpecker wouldn't really see it
   on the ground.

If a woodchuck pecked,
It would surely be a wreck,
Like a wooden-legged peckerwood writing
   a check.

How much wood could a woodpecker chuck,
If a peckerwood's a checkerboard square?
How much chuck would a peckerwood peck
If the checkerboard's just thin air?

If a chuckwagon wiggled
And a woodpecker sniggled,
Would a ham bone come from a hole in the
   middle?

If a woodchuck chucked
And a peckerwood ducked,
Could a woodpecker pick a wooden
  ten-ton truck?

And really . . . how much would a
  woodpecker care
If a peckerwood's a checkerboard square?

She finished the song, turned a smile on me,
and bowed. It appeared that I was supposed to . . .
well, clap or something. Applaud. Cheer. Okay, fine.
I was a guest in her cave and she'd sung a song for
me, so I could clap and cheer. However . . .

Tell the truth. Did that song seem strange to
you? It seemed very strange to me, and that was
sure too bad, because I was fixing to take a test on
it. Yipes.

I clapped and she bowed and smiled, then held
up her wings. "Thank you so much. Did you really
love my song?"

"Oh boy . . . uh . . . yes. You bet. Great song."

"The melody still isn't just right, but I love the
words."

"Absolutely. Great words. Very meaningful."

"Thank you, thank you. I would have been so
upset if you hadn't liked it."

"Oh no, it was . . . listen, Madame, about that little test . . ."

Once again, she flopped down and propped her head on her wing. "It isn't a *little* test. It's an enormous test, probably the most important test of your entire life."

I swallowed. "Oh? Gee. Well, what happens if I . . . well . . . flunk?"

"Oh dear. If you flunked the test, you'd have to go to Special Tutoring."

"Special Tutoring?"

"Yes. For five or six years, I should think."

"Five or six . . ."

"These things take time. But you'd have our very best tutor." She smiled. "Timothy."

"Timothy!" I rose to my feet and began looking around for an exit. There was only one way out, and Big Tim had slithered right into the middle of it. "Listen, Madame, I just remembered something. I need to be going, no kidding, and . . ."

She patted the air with her wing. "Sit down, O Rabbity Hank, and prepare for your test."

I slumped back down. My mouth was suddenly dry. "Madame, I'll be honest. That song of yours . . . it didn't make a lick of sense to me. It was all . . . gibberish."

"Well, of course, you silly rabbit! All my songs

are written in Gibberish. It's my native tongue. The whole purpose of the test is to see if you can translate the Gibberish into another language, such as . . . Flibberish."

"I never heard of it."

"Then this will be hard for you."

I rose to my feet. "Madame, I really need to be going."

"Timothy!"

Big Tim reared his head and began to rattle his tail. I sat down. "Okay, what the heck, let's take the test. What's the first question?"

"The question was contained in the song."

"You mean, 'how much wood could a wood-pecker . . .', all that stuff?" She nodded. "Oh brother. Can you give me a hint?"

She blinked her eyes and looked up at the ceiling. "Those roots get longer every year."

"Is that a hint?"

"No. I'm talking to myself. A hint. Very well, here's a hint. Use higher mathematics. Think of a word between one and ten. Choose a number that rhymes with chrysanthemum. And always remember: never shake the hand that bites you. Does that help?"

"No. It's more gibberish."

"Then trust your intuition, my dear boy. Intuition will save you when all else fails."

"Oh brother. Okay, I'll give it a shot."

This promised to be one of the toughest assignments of my whole career. It required Heavy Duty Thinking and also Extra Strength Mathematics. To get the right answer, I had to add up all the peckerwoods and woodpeckers, multiply that times the number of woodchucks, and then divide all that by checkerboards. Here, you want to see the equation?

$$\frac{(pw + wp) \times (wc)}{cb} = ??$$

Pretty impressive, huh? You bet it was. You're probably astounded that a dog could handle all that Extra Strength Mathematics. To tell you the truth, so was I. But the important thing is that I did it. Under great pressure and stress and so forth, after hours and hours of intense concentration, I finally came up with an answer. I could only hope it was the right one.

"Okay, Madame, I think I've worked this out. Madame?" She was asleep. "Hey, wake up! I've got the answer."

She sat up and yawned. When her eyes came into focus, she jumped up and yelled, "Timothy, come at once! Call out the guard, lock the outer doors! There's a giant rabbit in my office!"

In a flash, Big Tim was there beside me, rearing his ugly head, rattling his tail, hissing, and sticking out his tongue. I held my breath and didn't move a hair. It was a very tense moment.

Madame blinked her eyes and said, "Oh. Is that you?"

"Yes ma'am, it sure is. Will you call off your snake?"

"Timothy, at ease. We had a false alarm."

Big Tim gave me one last glare and slithered off into the darkness. I heaved a sigh of relief and turned to Madame. "I worked out the math and I think I've got the answer."

"Why did it take you so long?"

"Hey, it was a tough problem. Are you ready for this? The answer is . . ." I paused for dramatic effect. "97.001."

The cave fell into an eerie silence. Madame stared at me with eyes that looked like full moons. Her lower beak dropped two inches. Then, in a whisper, she said, "Astounding! Incredible! I can hardly believe it. Timothy, did you hear that? Oh Hank, it's true, you really are a genius!"

She hopped down to the floor and threw her wings around my neck. And she even kissed me

on the cheek. That was a new experience for me, being kissed by a woman who didn't have any lips. (She had a beak, don't you see, no lips.)

Anyway, I almost fainted with relief. We joined paws and wing tips (my paws, her wing tips) and danced around the cave, celebrating my . . . you know, Madame seemed surprised that I'd solved the problem and had turned out to be a mathematical genius, but, heck, I could have told her . . .

Anyway, we had a nice celebration, then Madame returned to her spot at the front of the cave. For a long time she stared at me with big adoring eyes. "Well, my dear boy, you've passed all the tests and surpassed all expectations. You've astounded us all with your brilliance. You've earned the right to proceed. The Path to Truth is open to you, and now you may ask my advice. What, pray tell, is the source of your troubles?"

I sat down and told her my sad story.

CHAPTER TWELVE

It Wasn't
a Space Robot

When I had poured it all out, she sighed, "Oh, this is so sad! You poor boy! All that work and devotion to duty, and nobody appreciated your sacrifices!"

"Yes ma'am, and here I am, alone in the wilderness, in exile, unloved and unwanted. Can you help me out of this mess? What *was* that thing in the garden?"

She drummed her claws and frowned. "You say the creature had a sharp nose and a long tail? Four legs and two ears? And body armor?"

"Right. And it made a clicking sound."

"Clicking sound. Hmmmm. This will be difficult." She closed her eyes and rocked back and forth. And she started mumbling some magic words:

116

"Oh, vapors, vapors, vanilla wafers,
Luminiferous ether tree.
Spiders, toads, and alligators,
Solve for us this mystery."

I watched and waited. Madame didn't move. Then her eyes slid open. "It didn't work. I've drawn a blank. The vapors were there, but they refused to reveal the answer. I'll try one more time:

Naughty vapors, hateful things,
Phantoms of the darkest pit.
Reveal to us the things we seek
Or I shall throw a hissy fit."

A smile slid across her beak. She opened her eyes and glanced around. "You know, I think that one worked."

"Great! What's the answer?"

Her smile faded. "Well, it was a little foggy. The name of the object begins with . . . an A. Then we have an R . . . and an M."

"A-R-M. Okay, we're making some . . . huh? Wait a minute, hold everything." I began pacing in front of her, as I often do when my mind is hot on the trail of a clue. "I'm beginning to see a pattern here, Madame. Does the word end with an O?"

"Let me check that." She consulted the vapors . . .

or whatever they were. "Yes, yes, it ends with an O. But how did you know that?"

"Heh. I have my ways, Madame. You're not the only one with amazing powers. Okay, we've got the first three letters and the last letter. What's the rest of it?"

She squeezed her eyes shut. "Let me see. Armarillo?"

"No, I've already tried that."

"Armatunafishio?"

"What? No. Keep probing, Madame, I think we're very close to something."

"Wait! Wait! There it is. Yes, I think I have it this time!" She opened her eyes, leaned forward, and whispered, *"It's an armadillo!"*

I stopped pacing . . . froze in my tracks, actually. "That's impossible. Armadillos live down south. We've never had an armadillo on our ranch."

She shrugged. "I'm sorry, but what can I say? You have an armadillo in your garden."

I cut my eyes from side to side. "Come to think of it, the clues do kind of fit together: small four-legged animal, sharp nose, no hair, long tail, armored plates. You know, Madame, I think we've just blown this case wide open. And you know what else? With this new information, I think I can get my job back. Thanks a million."

"Think nothing of it." She cocked her head to the side and gave me a puzzled look. "But you know, Hank, we never did work out the problem of your rabbitness. Are you a rabbit? Do you *think* you're a rabbit? Do I think you're a rabbit? Or is this all a delicious dream?"

"Some other time, Madame. I've got a case to finish. Many thanks for your help."

With that, I rushed to the entrance and wiggled my way outside. There, I found myself nose-to-nose with Big Tim. He flicked out his tongue. In a moment of impulse and great courage, I said, "Put that thing back in your mouth before you step on it."

Then, before he could respond, I roared away and left him to choke and sputter on my brilliant remark.

I told him, didn't I? Heh heh. Arrogant snake.

I pointed myself toward ranch headquarters and left the wilderness behind me—the wilderness and all its unhappy memories. I had survived my lonely exile, had gained the crucial piece of knowledge that would enable me to wrap up The Case of the Burrowing Robot, and now all I had to do was wrap it up.

An armadillo. Can you believe that? Who would have . . . you thought it was some kind of robotic device from another galaxy, right? Ha ha. Not me. Okay, for a short period of time, I had considered it one of the possibilities in the case, but only one of many, and not for very long. No kidding.

The important thing was that I had worked it out on my own—okay, with a smidgeon of help from Madame Moonshine—I had so-forthed the so forth virtually on my own, and Pete the Barncat's wild speculations about the case had been blown out of the water by the Torpedos of Truth.

The dumb cat. Imagine him trying to give ME advice about solving a case. Ha.

Anyways, we had us a new day started and I was feeling great as I roared into ranch headquarters. I throttled back on my powerful jet engines and executed a smooth landing, right in front of the garden.

Guess who or whom I found sitting beside the garden gate. Drover. I climbed out of the cockpit of my mind and went striding over to him. He looked up and gave me his usual silly grin.

"Oh, hi. Did you run out of eggs?"

"What?"

"You went to the Isle of Eggs, and I thought . . ."

"I went into exile, Drover, *exile*, and it had nothing to do with eggs. It had to do with suffering and a heroic journey into the bowls of the earth."

"Boy, I love bowls of eggs."

"And for your information, I've returned from my journey with the missing piece of the puzzle. I now know the true identity of that thing that was digging in the garden."

"An armadillo?"

"It was an *armadillo*, Drover, the first armadillo ever to set foot on this ranch."

"I'll be derned."

"It's just a pity that you didn't follow the clues to their logical extremities. It would have saved us a lot of time and embarrassment. Because of your bungling, the Security Division has suffered a terrible blow to its reputation."

"Yeah, and the wind blew all day."

"We can only hope it's not too late to redeem ourselves." I cast a glance into the garden. Everything appeared to be just as I had left it. "Did he ever come out?"

"Oh yeah. He's doing chores at the corral."

My gaze moved from the garden to Drover's empty eyes. "What? The armadillo is doing chores?"

"I thought you were asking about Slim."

"I was NOT asking about Slim. The armadillo, Drover, did he ever come out of his hole?"

"Well, let me think about that. I've been here since you left and . . . nope, I didn't see him."

"Great. He's still in the garden." I pushed my way past Drover. "As of this moment, you're relieved of duty. I'm taking command of this case."

"Fine with me."

"What? Speak up."

"I said . . . oh drat."

"I'm sorry, but it's time to put the first team back into the game." I marched up to the fence and jumped it as gracefully as a deer, then made my way over to the hole. I put my ear to the ground and listened.

Clicking. The rascal was still down there, only this time we had a plan for getting rid of him. I took a wide four-point stance and filled my lungs with fresh eggs . . . fresh air, let us say.

"Pay attention, son. I'm fixing to show you how we . . ."

ZOOM!

He was gone. Drover, that is. One second he was there, and the next he was streaking toward the machine shed. The little coward. Oh well, I didn't need him anyway.

I pointed my nose toward the hole and launched my plan of action. The plan was pretty simple. I would stand in front of the hole and bark until someone came to check out the disturbance. Then . . .

It worked slick. I had been barking only ten

minutes when I looked up and saw Slim, leaning against one of the gate posts. His arms were folded across his chest and he had a sour expression on his face.

"You know, pooch, we've already discussed you and the garden, and I think we decided you ain't welcome."

Yes, but this was a different deal. I lifted my ears, pointed my nose like a flaming arrow toward the hole, and barked.

"If I was you, I think I'd . . ." Slim looked closer. "Hank, you're looking kind of serious."

Right.

"Is something in that hole?"

These people require so much patience. YES!

He unslumped himself off the gate post and entered the garden, coming at his usual pace—slower than cold molasses. He bent down and listened. From deep inside the earth, he heard the clicking sound. His eyes grew wide.

"Well, I'll be derned. You don't reckon . . . Hank, I'll bet I know what that is! Son, you have just dumbed your way into a major discovery. That's an armadillo in there!"

Well, by George it had taken him long enough to figure it out. How many barks had I used up trying to get the point across to him? A hundred?

A thousand? And of course he had managed to scatter a few insulting remarks along the way.

Oh well. The important thing is that within fifteen minutes, we had the case wrapped up. Slim dug the armadillo out with posthole diggers, pulled him out by his tail, dropped him into a gunnysack,

and hauled him off to the north end of the ranch.

Better yet, Sally May showed up for the last five minutes of the procedure and realized that a terrible injustice had been done to the Head of Ranch Security. With tears streaming down both sides of her face, she threw her arms around my neck, begged me to forgive her for being such a crab, and invited me to join the family for a steak dinner in my honor.

Okay, maybe she . . . but she did apologize. That part's true.

So there you are. Once again, I had pulled the ranch through another dangerous time and had saved Sally May's garden from ruin and destruction.

Does it get any better than that? Not around here.

Case closed.

Oh, remember all that stuff about the robot from outer space? Ha ha. Nothing to it, just idle chatter. And if you want to, uh, remove those offensive passages from the book, that'll be okay with me. Thanks.

It was just an armadillo.

The following activities are samples from *The Hank Times*, the official newspaper of Hank's Security Force. Do not write on these pages unless this is your book. Even then, why not just find a scrap of paper?

Rhyme Time

S ally May decides she is tired of cleaning up after messy cowboys and dogs. She is going to get a new job. What jobs could she do?

Make a rhyme using the name "May" that would relate to the jobs below.

Example: Sally May could do horse impressions.
Sally May NEIGH

1. Sally May could have her own 24-hour period of time.

2. Sally May could teach dogs to sit and not move.

3. Sally May could buy a theater and put this kind of show on.

4. Sally May could buy the water inlet in San Francisco.

5. Sally May makes bales from this grass product found in pastures.

6. Sally May invents a new bathroom scale.

7. Sally May becomes a beam of sunlight.

8. Sally May owns a store where everything she sells is this one color.

9. Sally May invents a new type of this device for carrying school cafeteria lunch on.

Answers:

1. Sally May DAY
2. Sally May STAY
3. Sally May PLAY
4. Sally May BAY
5. Sally May HAY
6. Sally May
   WEIGH
7. Sally May RAY
8. Sally May GRAY
9. Sally May TRAY

Tropical Illusion

The drawings below may look the same; however, it is clearly a "tropical" illusion. A tropical illusion is something that isn't what it appears to be. Can you find the 11 differences between the two drawings? Circle each difference you find on the top drawing.

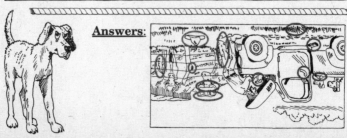

Answers:

"Photogenic" Memory Quiz

We all know that Hank has a "photogenic" memory—being aware of your surroundings is an important quality for a Head of Ranch Security. Now you can test your powers of observation.

How good is your memory? Look at the illustration on page 124 and try to remember as many things about it as possible. Then turn back to this page and see how many questions you can answer.

1. Was Slim holding the armadillo with his left hand or his right hand?

2. How many strands of barb wire were there—1, 2, or 3?

3. What was stuck in the ground next to Slim—a posthole digger, a shovel, or a rake?

4. Was Hank's tail pointing up or down?

5. Could you see Slim's belt buckle?

6. How many of Hank's eyes could you see—1 or 2?

Have you read all of Hank's adventures?

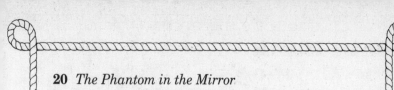

Join Hank the Cowdog's Security Force

Are you a big Hank the Cowdog fan? Then you'll want to join Hank's Security Force. Here is some of the neat stuff you will receive:

Welcome Package
- A Hank paperback of your choice
- A free Hank bookmark

Eight issues of *The Hank Times* newspaper
- Stories about Hank and his friends
- Lots of great games and puzzles
- Special previews of future books
- Fun contests

More Security Force Benefits
- Special discounts on Hank books and audiotapes
- An original Hank poster (19" x 25") absolutely free
- Unlimited access to Hank's Security Force website at www.hankthecowdog.com

Total value of the Welcome Package and *The Hank Times* is $23.95. However, your two-year membership is **only $8.95** plus $4.00 for shipping and handling.

- -

☐ Yes, I want to join Hank's Security Force. Enclosed is $12.95 ($8.95 + $4.00 for shipping and handling) for my **two-year membership**. [Make check payable to Maverick Books. International shipping extra.]

WHICH BOOK WOULD YOU LIKE TO RECEIVE IN YOUR WELCOME PACKAGE? CHOOSE ANY BOOK IN THE SERIES.

_____

                                                    BOY or GIRL
YOUR NAME   (CIRCLE ONE)

_____

MAILING ADDRESS

_____

CITY   STATE   ZIP

_____

TELEPHONE   BIRTH DATE
_____ Are you a ☐ Teacher or ☐ Librarian?
E-MAIL

Send check or money order for $12.95 to:

Hank's Security Force   **DO NOT SEND CASH.**
Maverick Books   **OFFER SUBJECT TO CHANGE.**
P.O. Box 549   *Allow 3–4 weeks for delivery.*
Perryton, Texas 79070

The Hank the Cowdog Security Force, the Welcome Package, and The Hank Times *are the sole responsibility of Maverick Books. They are not organized, sponsored, or endorsed by Penguin Group (USA) Inc., Puffin Books, Viking Children's Books, or their subsidiaries or affiliates.*